I0729060

When the Contralto Sings

Books in This Series

The Margarita Solution

Chiseler with a Glass Jaw

When the Contralto Sings

Stalking the Scratch Man

The Tenacious Goldbrick

Cryptic Paisley

When the Contralto Sings

When *the* Contralto Sings

Chester Henry

DAGMAR MIURA

LOS ANGELES

Published by Dagmar Miura
Los Angeles
www.dagmarmiura.com

When the Contralto Sings

Copyright © 2019, 2023 Dagmar Miura
All rights reserved. No part of this book may be used or reproduced in any manner whatsoever without prior written permission except in the case of brief quotations embodied in critical articles or reviews. For information, address Dagmar Miura, dagmarmiura@gmail.com, or visit our website at www.dagmarmiura.com.

This is a work of fiction. Names, characters, businesses, places, events, and incidents are either the products of the author's imagination or used in a fictitious manner. Any resemblance to actual persons, living or dead, or actual events is purely coincidental.

First published 2019

ISBN: 978-1-951130-07-7

ONE

It was probably just going to be a minor shake-down, Celeste thought, eyeing the homeless woman on the sidewalk, visible in the wan light of the streetlamp. She was clearly waiting for Celeste to step out of the car. She took a minute to adjust her hair in the rearview, but the woman stood her ground. Dressed in jeans and a dark nylon jacket that was torn around the shoulder, her expression was impassive, and patient, like she had all the time in the world. Pulling open the console, Celeste dug around and found a loose Ativan tablet, crunching it between her teeth before she opened the door.

"Good morning, miss," the woman began, flashing her a smile.

"It's evening," Celeste said. "The sun went

down an hour ago."

"But will it be a good morning? Will your car still be here then?" She raised her eyebrows. "I offer a unique service to make sure it stays safe."

Celeste glanced around the street. Technically this wasn't Skid Row, but LA's growing homeless problem had spread outward, and there were tents and sleeping bags on the sidewalks here, at the edge of the Fashion District. At this hour the retail storefronts and wholesale clothing businesses were all shuttered, the street quiet. There would be few witnesses if someone broke into her car. This woman wasn't physically intimidating—she was junkie-thin compared to Celeste's solid curvy frame—but that didn't mean the car would be safe.

"I understand the issue," Celeste said. "I'm just not sure whether I should pay you."

"The work I do is guaranteed. I'll be around until you get back."

"It's not that. My problem is that it sets a precedent. I don't live here, but I come here all the time."

"My services are available to residents and visitors alike." The woman absently brushed at her hair, even though adjusting it had no impact on her closely cropped Afro. There was some gray in it, Celeste saw. She looked to be in her forties.

"Let me call my friend Tru. He lives here."

She gestured to the brick building across the sidewalk and pulled out her phone. When Truman picked up, she said, "Can you come down to the street?"

A minute later Truman pushed out the front door. He was already dressed to go out, in a sharp fitted shirt and dark trousers, his thick brown hair carefully styled to look like it hadn't been styled.

"You're Truth?" the woman said to him. "You live in there?"

"It's Truman." He stepped toward her, subtly giving her the once-over.

"Fancy place."

"It's really not. It's commercial space with hard-lease units. It's like living in a warehouse."

"We're neighbors," she said, and gestured to the dark tent-filled alley that ran along the side of the building. "I live next door."

Truman nodded. Some of the other tenants in his building had been lobbying to get them cleared out, but the city had scant resources to do much more than address the most egregiously disruptive homeless encampments in places where the tourists went. This one wasn't like that, tucked mostly out of sight in a commercial district.

"Well, since we're neighbors," he said, "maybe Celeste could spare a dollar."

"Sure I can," she said, and dug in her pants pocket, handing her a single.

"Thank you, Celeste," she said, deftly pronouncing it the Spanish way, *suh-les-tay*. Even though Celeste had dark Latin coloring, and her shoulder-length hair was jet-black, lots of people Anglicized it to *suh-lest*. The dollar quickly disappeared into the woman's jeans.

"What's your name?" Celeste asked her.

"They call me Angel."

"That's sweet. So tonight you'll be the guardian angel for my ride."

She stepped toward Truman and the entrance to his building, but turned back when Angel spoke.

"You should come to the festival."

"What's that, exactly?" Celeste said.

"It's for Skid Row art and culture. It's in Gladys Park tomorrow. I'm performing."

"What kind of art?"

Watching Celeste react as her interest was piqued, Truman had to grin. Celeste worked in an art gallery, and was always looking for fresh ideas in that realm.

Angel bit her lip before she answered. "I guess it's Skid Row art. We had to get a permit and all that."

"Do you play an instrument?"

She laughed. "Angel is an instrument."

Celeste eyed Truman. "Do you know Gladys Park?"

"Sure—you can walk there from here. It's on Sixth. Right in the heart of Skid Row."

"Lots of the folks on the streets have talent," Angel said. "It's a showcase for us."

"It sounds like fun," Truman said.

Celeste asked Angel, "Do you think it'll be safe?"

"The place will be crawling with cops."

"Maybe we'll come by."

"You should," Angel said. "And thank you for your business, Celeste. Don't worry at all about your vehicle."

As she walked into the alley, Truman gestured to the little blue car. "We can just go."

"I wanted to make a withdrawal first."

"That's easy." Truman produced his keys and opened the front door, then started up the stairs to his loft.

"I never really checked out that alley," Celeste said, a few steps behind him. "It looks like there might be a lot of people camped there."

"When I moved here it was just an empty alley. Sometimes people would dump garbage, but now it's an encampment, and it's only getting worse."

"I totally misread the situation with Angel just now too."

"I wondered why you called for backup."

"I had it in my mind that it was a shakedown,"

she said. "I thought she'd want ten or fifteen bucks every time I came by, like parking in a paid lot. But a dollar per visit, I can handle."

"We should totally go to that festival," Truman said, unlocking his front door.

"If it's in the morning, sure. I have to work after."

A century ago the building Truman lived in had been put up as a warehouse, and it still had the brick walls and concrete floors. Truman's loft was on the upper floor, with a wooden lattice of rafters high overhead to hold up the roof. It was mostly one huge room, with three thrift-store sofas at one end arranged in a square to delineate a virtual living room. His desk sat under the high multipaned windows, and at the far side, past the kitchen counter and his bed, was the rack with all his clothes.

The only interior walls were the ones that Celeste's dad, Ernesto, had helped him build around the bathroom. Initially Truman had asked him to help rewire the place, as it only had a few high-voltage sockets for big machinery. Ernesto had been shocked that the toilet and shower weren't cordoned off. "What if you have guests, and somebody needs to use the head?" he'd said. So in addition to wiring the place so that his electronics and his coffeemaker would work, he'd helped Truman hammer together the framing and put up drywall around the space.

Truman took his aluminum stepladder from behind his clothes rack and set it up next to the bathroom wall, then climbed up a few steps. The walls ended eight feet up, which looked a bit strange, like there was a big white cube in the room. But Ernesto said extending the walls up the full fifteen feet to the rafters would look even stranger.

The tops of the bathroom walls were open, revealing the narrow gap between the inner and outer sheets of drywall. Truman had tied cords to socket wrenches that spanned the gap but were short enough not to be seen from below. It was the safest place he could think of to hide their cash. He reeled up one of the cords now to pull out the dusty canvas bag clipped to the other end, and tossed it down to Celeste.

Truman watched as she set it on the floor and zipped it open, revealing the bundles of cash bound with elastic bands. Sometimes he woke up in a cold sweat thinking about where the money had come from. On his first case as a detective, he'd swiped it from a couple of drug dealers who were about to export a whole duffel bag full of cash. Both of them had been arrested, and Truman had been left alone with the bag for a while. He'd left some of the money for the police to seize, and hopefully that meant whoever was expecting delivery of the duffel bag had written it off as lost to law enforcement. So far no one had connected it to him or Celeste. They were both extremely careful about how they spent it, and they limited how much they ran through the banks.

"Can you grab two grand or so for me?" Truman said.

Celeste riffled through the bills and then zipped the bag shut. "Do you care how much I took?"

"Not in the slightest."

She handed the bag up to him, and he clipped it onto the carabiner at the end of the cord again, then lowered it inside the wall, positioning the wrench so that the bag wouldn't fall to the bottom. Once he was down the ladder, he folded it shut and put it behind his clothes again, rolling the rack back into place. If someone broke in, no way did he want them climbing up there and discovering the stash. No one had ever done that, but it was always possible, and every day there were more homeless people around—and they had little left to lose.

Celeste handed him his cash, a wad of C-notes and twenties. He threw most of it in his desk drawer, tucking a few hundred into his pants.

"You got a little dusty," she said, and pointed to his shirt.

Truman took a moment to slap it off, then followed her out the door, pausing to lock the deadbolt. It was getting cold out, he realized, once they were down on the street, walking over to Celeste's car. Glancing into the alley, he wondered if Angel kept warm enough. This part of town was laid out on the Spanish colonial grid, with the streets running southwest to northeast to maximize sun exposure, but he knew that alley only got direct sunlight early in the morning.

"Latin boys?" Celeste said, stepping around to the driver's door.

"I love that place, although it's going to be crowded. Saturday is amateur night."

"It'll be worth it."

Celeste started the tinny little engine and flicked on the headlights, then navigated north, toward the central market and the bar they both loved. When they were close, Celeste stopped to let a car pull out of a street space, then nosed into it and killed the engine.

"Excellent parking karma," Truman said, and climbed out.

The place was already packed when they walked in, with house music thumping and lots of bodies under the pink lights on the dance floor. Through an archway farther back was a quieter space with the bar, and they maneuvered through the crowd to get there. This place had a great mix of people, gay and straight, loud and happy, with no pretense, and there were always lots of Latin guys.

"It's raining men," Truman said, raising his voice over the music.

Celeste laughed. "Hallelujah."

Truman let her push up to the bar to get drinks, as she was usually more successful at it under crowded conditions. She ordered him his standard margarita, and for herself a gin and tonic. When the harried bartender set the drinks down in front of her, she paid her with one of the dog-eared twenties she'd taken from their stash.

Holding the drinks high to avoid spilling them, she stepped over to where Truman was and handed him his margarita. They clinked glasses in a tacit toast and stood surveying the crowd as they drank.

Spotting a guy over Celeste's shoulder, Truman said, "Time to deploy the irresistible dichotomy."

It was a tactic they used to pick up guys—presenting themselves on an equal footing. In theory no man could resist the choice of one of them or the other. In practice they usually both got turned down, although each of them had scored a few make-out sessions.

Celeste subtly shifted position to get a look. The guy was tall, with buzz-cut hair, and he was wearing a dark uniform.

"What is your deal with cops?"

"He's not a cop," Truman said. "He's a security guard."

The guy noticed them looking at him, and greeted them affably. "Hey."

"We were just admiring your uniform," Truman said.

"We both were, equally," Celeste said.

He grinned. "I'm not here for that. I'm just having some fun with my friends."

"I'm sorry to hear that," Celeste said, holding his gaze and swirling the ice in her highball glass.

"It is a little sad," Truman added.

The guy laughed, showing a toothy smile. "You two need to loosen up. This place is for fun, not for hookups."

"I appreciate the clarification, officer," Celeste said, and turned away. She leaned toward Truman. "It's actually for both, right?"

"Totally. But he's got a point—we don't need to be on the make all the time."

"I'm going to dance."

She handed him her nearly empty glass and pushed her way toward the dance floor. Truman watched as she bopped and shimmied, bouncing around among the other bodies, and grinned at her exuberance.

Not far away a guy caught his eye and held it

for a moment. Truman nodded and looked him over. He had great hair, dark and sleekly styled, and he was young—maybe even too young to be in here.

The guy stepped over and said, "Hey."

They talked for a while, as Truman sipped the icy dregs of his margarita. It wasn't even clear that the guy was flirting. Maybe he was just happy to be out with people on a Saturday night.

Eventually the guy wandered off, and Celeste returned, looking happy but worn out.

"Ready to go?" she said, pushing her hair back.

Truman nodded in assent and followed her toward the entrance.

Once they were out on the street, Celeste said, "It's cold out here."

"That's because you're sweating."

They climbed into the car, and Celeste navigated back toward the Fashion District.

"That was better than any gym workout," she said, braking for a red light.

"Definitely more fun too."

"The music was really great tonight."

Truman eyed her. Was she on something more than gin and good music? A while back he'd confronted her about her drug use, and she'd promised to work on getting clean, but it was hard even to talk about it with her.

When Celeste pulled up outside his building,

Truman popped the door handle and turned to her before he got out. "Gladys Park in the morning?"

"Definitely. I always enjoy art more when it can't easily be summarized in words."

Truman chuckled. "I'm not sure if that's about the content of the event or about how Angel's mind works."

As he unlocked the entry door, he heard the little engine rev as Celeste pulled out. That had been a strong margarita, and he was still a little buzzed, he realized when he got upstairs. He downed a big glass of water, and peeled off his clothes, then doused the lights. After he climbed into bed, he gazed at the glow of the city outside the high windows. Thinking about Celeste's drug use, he felt a twinge of guilt. Maybe he was being judgmental. Maybe it was old news, and she was totally sober now, and he was just being paranoid.

TWO

In the morning, when Celeste parked in front of Truman's building, the neighborhood was crowded with vehicles and alive with foot traffic, the shutters on the shops and warehouses rolled open. The alley was in the shadow of Truman's building, but there was enough daylight that Celeste could see the tops of a dozen or more tents along its length. There was no sign of Angel, or anyone else. But Angel would be at the festival already.

Digging in the center console, Celeste found a Vicodin tablet and bit it in half, dropping the other part of it back in and grimacing at the bitterness as she crunched it between her teeth. She climbed out of the car and went to the building's entrance to ring Truman's buzzer.

"Ready to go?" she said when he answered.

"Come up," he said, the words broken by static, and the lock buzzed open.

Upstairs, Truman flipped the deadbolt open, then hustled over to his clothes rack to pull on a T-shirt and a pair of boxer shorts. When Celeste came in, she was dressed for work, in a white sleeveless blouse and a skirt.

"Did you just wake up?" she said, looking him over.

"I forgot to set my alarm. Want an espresso?"

"Hit me."

Truman fired up the espresso machine and tapped the grounds from yesterday into the garbage, then rinsed the filter and pressed in a scoop of fresh coffee.

"I slept like a log," Celeste called to him, settling into the most comfortable of the three sofas, the purple one against the wall.

"Not surprising. You were dancing like a wild thing."

Truman poured the coffee into two little demitasse cups and carried them over to the sofas, handing her one and slurping at the other. Walking over to his clothes rack, he pulled off his T-shirt and shorts and got dressed, in a polo shirt and gray jeans. After he buckled his belt, he finished the espresso and took the cup to the sink.

"I'm ready."

Celeste rose, and set her cup in the sink too, and Truman followed her out, locking the door behind him.

"Am I overdressed?" she said, as they descended the stairs.

"You look fine. I don't think you have to look homeless to go to a homeless festival."

On the street the temperature was perfect. In May and June the marine layer covered the basin until early afternoon, muting the sunlight. In a month or so it would be gone and the city would get seriously hot and cranky, but right now things were warm and mellow and comfortable.

"Should we walk?" Truman said.

"I looked up where the park was—it's so close to the gallery. We'll drive, and you can walk back."

They climbed into the little blue car and drove the few blocks to Sixth. Near the venue, Celeste found a space on a quiet side street that was heavily strewn with garbage. The opposite sidewalk was lined with tents and shopping carts piled with black plastic bags.

"It doesn't really feel safe," she said, but backed into the space anyway.

"It'll be OK for a short time. You're not leaving it here overnight."

They climbed out and walked back to the boulevard and around the corner. Gladys Park was tiny, and bleak, and mostly paved in concrete. People were crowded into the space, and on the sidewalk, and spilling into the street.

"Where's the park?" Celeste demanded.

"You're looking at it."

"It's more like a parking lot."

"I guess it's what you'd call an inner-city park."

A stage was set up at one side of the space, and it looked like a performance was happening. There was no seating, so they wandered closer, deeper into the crowd, to hear what was going on. Three performers were talking to each other, but with no amplification it was difficult to hear their dialogue.

Celeste folded her arms and tilted her head toward Truman. "It's hard to get the gist of it."

"All I'm getting is that it's vignettes about life on the streets."

Suddenly the actors' voices rose, and they got into a realistic shouting match over a patch of the stage. There was some shoving, but no punches thrown, and then it ended—the three actors broke character, and smiled at the spectators, and took a bow.

"I wasn't sure if that was a real disagreement or not," Celeste said, clapping with the rest of the audience as the trio trotted off stage.

"That means they're exceptionally skilled actors."

"Or that art and reality intersect on Skid Row."

As the actors left the stage, a guy with a wild mane of gray hair stepped out.

"Next up is one of our favorite bands, so give it up," he said, and walked off again, to a smattering of applause.

"What's the name of the band?" Celeste said.

"He totally forgot to say."

As they watched, the performers gradually appeared. First a rail-thin guy in a black T-shirt sat behind the drum kit, then two guys with brass instruments wandered out. One wore a natty bowling shirt and a straw fedora, but the other wore a grubby T-shirt and torn denim. Next came a woman in a long cotton dress wielding an electric guitar. She plugged it into an amp, and they all spent a minute tuning up.

Another woman stepped onto the stage and stood at the mic, adjusting its height. In a red top and black trousers, her long wavy hair spilled over her shoulders.

"That's Angel," Celeste said.

Truman peered at her. "You're right. Why does she look so different?"

"She's wearing a wig. Last night she had short natural hair."

The band started up and found a rhythm, and Angel embraced the mic. Her voice was clear, and pure, and on key:

> Don't let the devil drive your car
> 'Cause if you do, he'll take you too far
> Don't let him in

"She's got an amazing voice," Truman said, grinning as he watched her.

"She really does. Contraltos are the best."

"Is that the key she's singing in?"

"It's not about the music—it's her vocal range. To me contraltos are more real. Sopranos always sound affected."

"How do you know about vocal range?"

"I did a unit about opera music," Celeste said, her eyes on the stage. "It was an elective, but it falls under art history. Vocal range applies to any kind of music, like this stuff."

"They're all really good. The guy with the trumpet is a total boss."

"Why are they homeless? With that kind of talent, they could be working."

Truman shook his head. "It's a mystery."

"This piece is kind of jazzy, but it's about the devil—is it gospel music?"

"I know this song. I'd call it R&B. There are actually a bunch of different verses, but Angel is singing the same two over and over."

"I wondered about that."

After the number ended, and the band did two more sprawling extended songs, Angel smiled and threw up a hand in a big wave, then walked off stage to lots of applause. Truman clapped as loud as he could, and Celeste cupped her hands at her mouth to belt out a loud whoop.

The guitarist unplugged and left the stage with the trumpet player, and soon the only one left was the drummer, sweating and grinning and still futzing with his sticks. The shaggy emcee came back on stage and was about to speak when the drummer suddenly started playing louder. The emcee stepped toward the drums and leaned in to talk to him. At first the guy stopped, but then he played a little more, scowling at the emcee, who raised his voice in response. Another man in a black T-shirt came up to talk to them, animatedly waving his arms as they tried to reason with the drummer.

"What's up with that guy?" Truman said. "He doesn't look high to me."

"I don't think it's about drugs—he just can't follow the plot. Maybe he has some other impairment, like a disability. It could account for some of the mystery around their employment potential."

"That might be the deal with Angel too," Truman said. "She wasn't high last night, but she wasn't completely ordinary either."

Celeste looked around the park. "I was hoping for some visual art, but nada. Let's go look at the food vendors."

As they walked toward the row of carts along

the sidewalk, a woman stepped in front of them and pointed at Celeste's chunky black flats.

"Those are my shoes."

Celeste stopped short and frowned. "No they're not."

Truman looked the woman over. Her head was wrapped in orange fabric, a makeshift turban, and she was wearing a dark quilted jacket, even though the day was too warm for it. Her sneakers were the biggest giveaway that she was living on the streets—they were grubby and worn, and the left one was held together by a twisted length of wire rather than a lace.

"She's wearing my shoes," the woman said, raising her voice.

Celeste matched her volume. "You're wearing your own shoes."

"You took my stuff," the woman shouted.

A guy came up and stood almost between them, and Celeste took half a step back to make space. He was a little shorter than Celeste, and wore jeans and a collarless green dashiki that revealed his pleasingly developed pecs. His twisty black hair was short on the sides and knobby on top.

He smiled at the woman with the head wrap and spoke calmly. "It doesn't matter whose shoes they are. She's wearing them now. You have to let it go."

"They're my shoes," she insisted.

"So whose shoes are you wearing?"

She looked down at her feet, distracted for a moment, then looked up again and pointed at Celeste. "She went into my stuff."

A few paces away stood a uniformed cop, her hair in a tight bundle. She didn't look too concerned, and kept her distance, but she had definitely tuned in to the interaction, and was eyeing them all. The woman with the head wrap noticed her, glancing at her sidelong, and pressed her mouth into a tight line.

"Come and see me," the guy said to her. "We'll get you some new shoes. You know where to find me."

She jabbed a finger at Celeste. "Don't touch my stuff," she growled, then stalked off, in the direction opposite where the cop was standing.

Celeste watched her leave. "Phew. I thought I was going to have to walk around barefoot." She turned to the guy. "You really know how to talk to people. Thanks for stepping in."

"No problem," he said, raising his eyebrows, "but you really shouldn't have taken her stuff."

Celeste recoiled visibly, and the guy smiled.

"I'm just messing with you."

"How long have you been on the streets?" Truman said.

"I'm not homeless," he said, and laughed. "I'm

here a lot, though—I work at a Skid Row services provider. The name is Dyson."

Truman told him his name, and Dyson turned to Celeste to introduce himself to her too.

"I really can get her some shoes," Dyson said. "Usually we do that when we're trying to hook people up with job interviews."

"Is that your gig?" Celeste said. "Employment?"

"Correct."

"Do you find jobs for a lot of people?" Truman said.

"Not as many as I'd like, but enough to keep me engaged. The bigger problem is housing. Lots of these people work full-time and still can't afford a place to live. It's starting to feel like an insoluble problem."

"How many times did we vote to tax ourselves to fix this?" Truman said.

"It's going to take more than voting, brother." He looked to Celeste. "Do you two live around here?"

"Truman does, but not me. I work in a gallery in the Arts District." She gestured vaguely toward the street. "It's a couple blocks the other side of Alameda."

Dyson looked at Truman, his brow furrowing in mock concern. "And how long have you been on the streets?"

"I'm not—at least not yet."

"He exaggerates," Celeste said. "He's not really vulnerable. Truman is a well-paid detective."

Dyson's eyebrows shot up. "Seriously?"

Truman shrugged. "It's what I do."

"He has a guidebook and everything," Celeste said.

Truman shot her a look. He did use the deep well of wisdom in Biff Sturgis's *Eleven Steps to Becoming a Hard-Nosed Detective*, even though it had been written many decades ago, but like Biff said, a lot of the work couldn't be put down in words—you needed seasoned gut instinct.

"I should hire you," Dyson said. "I recently had something stolen from me."

"What was it?"

"A book. It was one of a kind."

"I can look into it for you," Truman said. "I'm not really busy right now."

"I can't afford to pay you much."

Truman furrowed his brow. "You need to ask yourself, how much is the book worth to you? Can you afford not to pay me?"

Dyson turned to Celeste. "Your boyfriend runs a good marketing game."

"Oh, god," she said, and waved a hand. "We're just friends."

Dyson eyed Truman for a moment. "Would you take the job for a maximum payment of seven hundred?"

Biff Sturgis had written a whole section about how to negotiate rates, and when to ask for cash up front, and how to make sure you got paid. But this guy had started high.

"I can try," Truman said. "Is that the replacement value of the book?"

"It's worth much more than that to me. Maybe you could drop by my office and I'll tell you about it. I work right over there, on Los Angeles Street."

Dyson gave him the address, and Truman pulled out his phone and thumb-typed it into a note.

"What's your phone number?" Truman said. After Dyson recited it, he added, "I just texted you mine."

"The festival is supposed to wind up at two sharp," Dyson said, "but on Skid Row time, it'll be more like three. Do you want to come over after that?"

"I'll be there."

After he'd said good-bye, Celeste watched him leave. "He was so into you."

"You think?"

"You couldn't tell? He hardly glanced at me, except to ask indirectly whether I was your girlfriend. But he checked out every inch of you—from your sneakers to your cheap haircut."

Truman laughed. "You're jealous."

"I'm not. I'm just not sure whether he really wants to hire you or just wanted to get your phone number."

Truman shrugged. "Either way."

Angel walked up to them, still wearing her long hair, a big smile on her face, and put a hand on each of their shoulders. "Hey, neighbors—you made it."

"You have an amazing voice," Celeste said.

Angel beamed and preened a little, snapping her fingers and shuffling her feet. "Thank you."

"Celeste says you're a contralto," Truman said.

"That's exactly right. Do you sing, sweetheart?"

"I don't," Celeste said, "but I learned a little about music in school."

"My home girl Marian Anderson was a contralto."

"Did you know her?" Celeste said, raising her eyebrows.

"I never met Ms. Marian, but she was my role model. I'd love to sound that polished."

"You totally do."

"Do you perform regularly with those musicians?" Truman said.

"Once in a while. When we're in the same place." Angel grinned. "We're not really organized as a band, so it's an unofficial association."

"I get it," Celeste said. "Are you singing again today?"

"Not me, but there are some other musicians on later." She squeezed Celeste's arm. "I'm going to talk to my people. Thanks for coming out."

Once she was gone, Celeste said, "I should go to work."

"I've seen enough too. I'll walk you to your car."

"Excellent," she said. "With a bodyguard, I might make it all the way there without getting mugged for my shoes."

Truman walked with her to the street and toward the corner. "Dyson is kind of sweet. I guess I'd do him."

"I know you didn't have to think about that."

He chuckled. "OK, but I wanted you to think that I did."

Celeste stepped around to the driver's side of her car. "If he's serious about hiring you, get that settled before you sleep with him. Otherwise he'll think you'll work for free."

Truman waved as she pulled out, then walked back to his loft. Once he was upstairs, he made another espresso and then sat at his desk and pulled open his laptop. A search for the street address Dyson had given him brought up a page for his agency, and Truman read through it as he sipped his coffee.

The nonprofit trained people for job interviews, and got them appropriate clothes for work, as Dyson had said. The group set up interviews with employers and also helped people do that themselves, providing a mailing address and a callback number for people without a phone.

Dyson's name was listed among the staff with the job title "counselor." When he'd introduced himself, it hadn't been clear whether Dyson was a first name, or a family name, or a nickname, but the site listed him as Dyson Norris. Truman didn't even have to write that down; it was easy to remember.

A while later he checked the time—Dyson should be back in his office. He loaded a notepad into his backpack and slung it on, then headed down to the street.

THREE

The marine layer had burned off, and it felt warmer. Commerce was winding down for the day, with some of the businesses already closed, the streets quieter now than earlier. Dyson's office was farther west, right at the edge of Skid Row, just before the Historic Core, a few blocks of grand hundred-year-old office buildings that had been gentrified into housing and upscale retail. In the space of a single block, the transition was dramatic, from tents and trash to hip eateries and boutiques, and Dyson's office straddled the boundary.

Truman found the building, with the nonprofit's name plastered on the glass, and tried the door. It was locked, maybe because it was Sunday. He cupped his hands around his eyes and leaned in to peer inside. A moment later the door lock buzzed, and he pulled it open.

Inside, the space was modern and spare, with an expanse of gray carpeting but no furniture apart from the reception desk. A guy with a high hairline and a trim beard was parked behind it.

"Can I help you?" he said tentatively.

"I have a meeting with Dyson Norris."

He frowned and looked down at his desk, then carefully picked up the telephone receiver, gingerly holding it between his thumb and forefinger. Maybe he thought it was dirty, Truman reasoned. He pecked at the number pad with his other hand and spoke loudly into the mouthpiece, holding it well away from his head.

"You have a client," he said, and quickly replaced the receiver.

A moment later Dyson appeared from the hallway leading into the back and smiled at the sight of him.

"Come on in," he said.

"He'll need a haircut," the receptionist said. "I have those haircut coupons."

"Thanks, Mike," Dyson said. "I'll keep that in mind."

Truman followed him down the hall and into a tiny office with no windows. It was just big enough for the desk, a couple of chairs, and a file cabinet. Stacks of paperwork cluttered the surfaces.

"I just got my hair cut," Truman said, self-consciously running a hand through it as he stepped in after him.

"It looks fine to me, but I guess it's not up to Mike's standard. Although Mike is also afraid of electricity."

"Was he a client?"

"Good deduction. You really are a detective." Dyson closed his office door and waved at the chair in front of his desk. "Sit down."

"Why do you have office hours on Sunday?" Truman said, setting his bag on the floor as he dropped into the chair.

"We try to stay open every day, and evenings sometimes. Some of our clients have other jobs, or they're in classes. So how long have you been a detective?"

"A while now," Truman hedged.

"That means you're fairly new at it."

"That's accurate. I've solved a few cases, though—all the ones I've been hired to work on."

"What did you do before that?"

"I was a tour guide. I remember Gladys Park was a drive-by on one of the bus tours." In the deeper tone and careful enunciation he used when he'd worked as a guide, he recited the line from the script: "'Gladys Park is ground zero for Skid Row, the heart of LA's homelessness crisis.'"

Dyson laughed. "Concise yet informative."

Reaching into his backpack, Truman pulled out his notepad and dug for a pen. "So you lost a book. Where did you last see it?"

"Right here in my desk."

"In the drawer? Was it locked?"

"There's no lock. I should have put it in the file cabinet—I have a key to that. I didn't think anyone would come in to rifle my desk. Mostly people here respect each other."

Truman glanced at the door handle. It didn't have a bolt or any locking mechanism. "I see your office doesn't lock either. Do you think it was a client, or a staff member?"

"It has to be one or the other." He sighed. "More likely it was a client. It happened yesterday, when I wasn't here."

Truman looked around the ceiling. "No cameras?"

"Only in the front office."

"What's the name of the book?"

"It's called *Saucers over the Southwest*. It's about UFOs. The dust jacket is red with white lettering, and the binding is dark red. It's a hardcover, and it's huge." Dyson held his thumb and forefinger wide apart. "I can't remember the author's name, but it's from the 1980s."

Truman glanced up from making notes. "Is your name in it?"

"Not mine, but it has a bookplate inside the

front cover with a previous owner's. It's an *O* name, like O'Connor or O'Dowd. I can't remember exactly. But the bookplate has a full-color reproduction of *The Birth of Venus* by Botticelli. That's the one where she's a redhead, standing on a scallop shell, mostly naked but covering her cooter."

Truman chuckled. "I think I know it. Are you a UFO nut?"

"In a way, I suppose. I'm interested in science and paranormal stuff like flying saucers and UFOs."

"You make it sound like those are two different things."

Dyson sat forward, his gaze intent. "*UFO* means unidentified, right, so it could be anything. Just lights in the sky. A flying saucer is a tangible object—a spacecraft."

Truman raised his eyebrows. "Flown by aliens?"

"They might not be from other planets. They could be from other dimensions, right next to ours, or they might come from other times—they might be future descendants of us."

Truman frowned thoughtfully, watching him speak.

"You think I'm nuts."

"Not at all," Truman said. "I'm absorbing the ideas. Time-traveling flying saucers. I'm worried that you're going to blow my mind."

Dyson laughed, a deep guffaw, and leaned back in his chair.

"So this book is important to you."

"It has some annotations that I'd hate to lose. I need to get it back."

On his notepad, Truman wrote "Annotations?" He wasn't going to press Dyson on why the book was significant. Truman might not need to know that. But hiring him to retrieve some margin notes sounded implausible.

"Is there anyone in the office that you suspect?"

Dyson slowly shook his head. "I asked everyone on staff, in case someone borrowed it to read and planned to return it later. Some of them are a little offbeat, but no one has animus toward me. No one who works here would need the money they'd get by selling it either."

"Did you study psychology?"

"How did you know?"

"The language you use. What about your clients?"

"That's a whole other story." Dyson sighed. "They're all people with cash-flow problems, and lots have addiction problems. I've seen people in here having schizophrenic meltdowns."

"Do you have a record of who was here yesterday?"

"I checked the appointments list. It's about a dozen people. I have their street names, and some have phone numbers. But there are always others who come and go without appointments, so they won't be on any list."

"Can you send me what you have?"

Dyson sat up and looked at his computer screen. "What's your email?"

Truman rattled it off as he typed.

"What about the footage from the lobby?" Dyson said. "I made sure we saved the files for yesterday. I could go through it with you to identify people."

"Let's hold off on that for now." Truman tucked his notepad into his bag and lifted it into his lap. "I have some other ideas to start with."

"Do you need some money today?"

"We can deal with that later."

"A trusting man," Dyson said, raising his eyebrows. "That's rare."

Truman rose and slung on his backpack. "Don't mistake trusting for stupid."

"Of course not." Dyson got up and opened the door, then walked him to the lobby and shook his hand.

"I'll be in touch," Truman said.

"Do you need a haircut coupon?" Mike called to him from the reception desk.

"I appreciate the offer," Truman said, "but not today."

On the walk back to his loft, Truman was lost

in thought when his phone buzzed in his pants. It was an email from Dyson, he saw, with an image of Saturday's appointment list.

Dyson had called him trusting, but that's not what it was about. Truman might not be able to ask him for any dough at all if he couldn't get a lead. Hard-nosed Biff Sturgis said the client has to pay you for your work no matter what the outcome, but Truman's thinking was more nuanced. The initial approach he had in mind wouldn't consume that much of his time, so if he failed, and didn't earn anything, it wouldn't sting that much.

Up in his loft, he took out his notes and sat at his desk, then pulled open his laptop to do some digging online. *Saucers over the Southwest* had only been printed once, and only in hardcover, he found, but there were lots of copies for sale at used-book vendors around the country.

Next he looked up *The Birth of Venus*. He recognized the image, although he'd never noticed that she was portrayed as a redhead. Dyson was right—she was coyly covering her crotch with her long hair.

Folding his computer closed, Truman went over to his bookcase. It was taller than he was, but standing on its own against the expansive wall, it looked like doll furniture. There weren't many books on it—just enough to fill the lowest few shelves. He needed one that looked expensive, and he knelt on the concrete floor to study the spines. Finally he pulled out a thick hardback biography of John Adams. Its dust jacket was embossed with gold lettering. This would work perfectly—he wasn't going to read it again. Rising, he tucked it into his backpack and went down to the street.

Twilight was looming, and the alley next to his building was in deep shadow. He was leery of walking in there, among the tents and grocery carts and piled-up bags and boxes. It was hard to tell what was trash and what were valued possessions. Stepping into the path in the middle of the alley, he was hit with the sharp tang of homelessness, reminiscent of ammonia and vinegar, powerful here even though nobody was in sight. More than anything it was depressing to see this. The grim thought struck him that a few slow business months could put him out here too.

"Hello?" he called.

A man stood up from a tent a few yards farther along. He had a shaggy brown beard and his hair was tied back. "What do you want, Sunshine?"

"I'm looking for Angel."

"You know, I'm not exactly sure who that is. What do you want with her?"

"I know she lives here. I saw her at Gladys Park this morning."

The guy craned his neck and shouted into the

air. "Angel—show yourself."

No reply came, although a man's muffled voice called back, "Pipe down."

He met Truman's gaze and shrugged. "She's not here."

"What's your name?"

"They call me Beretta. Would sir care to leave a message?"

"I live next door. Tell her Truman is looking for her."

"There's a small service fee for relaying that kind of information."

"Put it on my tab."

Beretta scoffed and disappeared into his tent. As Truman walked back toward the street, his phone buzzed in his pants. It was a text from Celeste:

Where are you?

He thumb-typed a quick response:

Home.

Her reply came as he approached the sidewalk:

I just rang your doorbell.

Stepping around to the front entrance, he found Celeste in the fading daylight, gazing at her phone, her face illuminated by its blue glow.

She looked up in surprise when he emerged

from the alley. "Hanging out with your new friends?"

"I asked my man Beretta to send Angel over," Truman said, and moved to unlock the front door.

"Why?"

As they climbed the stairs and went into his loft, Truman explained his meeting with Dyson, and the plan he'd formulated. Celeste went over to his fridge and scanned the contents.

"You're out of cherry," she called to him, taking one of the Italian sodas. "That's the best kind." She pausing at the counter to find the bottle opener and pop off the cap.

Truman set his backpack on the coffee table and sat on one of the sofas, arms spread along the back, waiting for her.

"That's quite the street name," Celeste said, settling on an adjacent sofa. "Beretta. I wonder if it means he's armed?"

"I hope not."

"Stray bullets tend to do strange things. They won't come through your walls. The bricks will stop them. But a bullet would go through your windows like they weren't even there."

"Great," he said flatly.

"So is he cute?"

"Beretta? In a way, but he's not for me."

"That's a relief. It's a bad idea to sleep with homeless people."

Truman chuckled. "Is that wisdom from personal experience?"

"It just seems like a fast track to having a live-in boyfriend," she said, and sipped her soda. "So what was Dyson's office like?"

"Small," Truman said. "It's a nonprofit, and it seems like they're doing useful work. Like he told us, the focus is helping dysfunctional people get jobs."

"What kind of book did he lose?"

"It's about UFOs. *Saucers over the Southwest.*"

She threw up a hand. "How cool is that?"

"He says he's interested in the subject, but he's not a UFO nut. There's a bookplate inside the front cover that's illustrated with *The Birth of Venus.* That's the one where she's standing on a scallop shell and hiding her cha-cha with her long red hair."

"I know it well. Did you look at the woman beside her? She's floating in the air, poised to throw a robe over Venus. Her own modesty isn't enough—she wants to completely obscure her nudity."

"I didn't notice that," Truman said, and pulled out his phone to find the image, then zoomed in on it. "You're right—I see it now."

"The cover-up is about the morals of Botticelli's time. The Romans wouldn't have tried to hide the perfect body of their goddess of beauty and sex. It's also odd that she's standing on a shell. The story is that she rose out of the sea foam."

"The mileage you get from that art history degree," Truman said, tucking his phone away.

Celeste waved a hand. "Surely Dyson's book isn't valuable because of the bookplate."

"Right. It's old, but it would be easy to replace it for thirty bucks, and you can buy a pristine copy online for around a hundred. So his copy has to be valuable for some reason."

"Did you ask him about that?"

"He says he needs to get his annotations back, but that doesn't make sense," Truman said. "You don't spend hundreds of dollars to get that specific copy—you spend a few hours reading the thirty-dollar replacement and making new notes."

"Maybe he wrote an important phone number in it, or a password, or the combination to a safe."

"Maybe. But the question is, what is he up to?"

"Should you really be suspicious of your client?"

"I'll do what he's paying me to do, but I'm pretty sure that he's lying to me about why he wants it back."

"I'm sure you'll figure it out," Celeste said, setting her bottle on the coffee table. "So—drinks. Do you want to go to that place with the turbines? I'm basically dressed for it."

"Every guy who steps in there is in a suit,"

Truman said. "Give me a minute to spiff up."

Over at his clothes rack, Truman changed into black dress pants and a dark-blue shirt, loosely knotting a mustard-yellow necktie at the collar. When they went down to the street and got into Celeste's car, there was no sign of Angel, or anyone else from the alley.

The bar Celeste wanted to go to wasn't far, in the Civic Center, and Celeste found a parking spot a block away. Down a flight of stairs in a basement, the place had been an electric substation a century ago, and it still retained its 1920s vibe. The space was glamorous but the drinks were expensive.

Strolling toward the bar, Celeste said, "It seems busy for a Sunday."

"I call Sunday a shoulder evening. Not a peak night, but not a slow night. It's when the more dedicated of the amateurs are out working on becoming barflies."

"Tru," she said firmly, "we are not barflies." She turned to the bartender. "A blended margarita for the man, and bring me a small of a pale lager."

"Will Kronenbourg work?"

"Fine," she said flatly. "Boring, but fine."

When he set the drinks down, Celeste set a twenty on the bar.

"It's twenty-four fifty."

"Ouch," Celeste said, and plunked down another twenty. As the bartender turned away to make change, she said to Truman, "Good thing I'm driving. I can't afford more than one."

"I'm sure the beer wasn't the expensive part. I should know better than to order a cocktail in a place like this." Truman tapped his glass against Celeste's and then slurped at it.

A couple of women got up from their barstools, and Truman went to claim the open seats, leaning back on the bar and facing the room. Once Celeste was perched on the adjacent stool, the guy on her other side leaned in to talk to her. Truman subtly checked him out. His hair was short and spiky, and he wore a rumpled gray suit. That meant he wore it all day, so he probably worked around here—a civil servant. He must not be too drunk, because Celeste engaged with him, and they chatted, and she laughed at something he said.

Truman sipped his margarita and people-watched. There was some eye candy, but the crowd trended toward straights, so this wasn't a place where guys flirted with him. It didn't always need to be about that, he reminded himself. It felt good just to be out.

When he'd finished his margarita, Celeste gave him the high sign. The guy she'd been talking to had disappeared. Truman slid off the stool, walking with her to the stairs.

Once they were out on the street, walking back to the car in the crisp evening air, Truman said, "There were no guys in there."

Celeste laughed. "Not for you, anyway."

"What was he like?"

"Not a keeper. Too full of himself. He didn't ask me anything about me, but I can tell you a dozen things about him."

"That's never a good pattern. Let me guess: he's a lawyer."

She eyed him sidelong. "How did you know?"

"You said he was full of himself, and he obviously lives in that suit."

"At least he's a public defender. That puts him on the less sleazy end of the spectrum."

"Don't they have to do that?" Truman said, climbing into the car.

"What do you mean?"

"I'm pretty sure law firms, or maybe it's the bar association, make them work as public defenders for a while. It's like forced charity work. I don't think they do it because they want to."

Celeste scoffed and started the engine. "I'm glad I threw him back."

———◆———

When they pulled up to Truman's building, Angel was sitting on the step in front of the door, wearing her dark jacket. Celeste killed the engine, and they both climbed out.

"Hey, pretty girl," Angel said, standing up. "Hey, Sunshine. I didn't know which bell was yours, so I rang all of them. You didn't answer any of them."

"Mine is the one labeled 'Boudreaux.'"

"Is that your name? That's a big one in Louisiana. Some of my people are from over that way. From the Big Easy. The Cajuns are mostly around Lafayette."

"I don't think my relatives with that name were Cajuns. They came from Massachusetts." Truman lowered his voice, as if sharing a confidence. "Listen—I wanted to ask if you could help me out. I've got a small job for you."

"Depends on what it is."

"I want you to sell something for me."

"Drugs?" Angel demanded.

"Nothing like that. Let me go grab it."

Truman unlocked the front door to his building and stepped inside. Angel turned to Celeste.

"That sweet boy doesn't look like a drug dealer."

"He's not. I've never seen him on anything stronger than tequila."

"You two are all dressed up. Were you out on the town?"

"We went to a bar over by the Civic Center."

"Ooh là là—sounds fancy. But you look pretty sober."

"The drinks were too expensive to get tight."

Angel cackled. "I hear you."

Truman came back outside a minute later and handed the John Adams book to Angel.

"Where am I supposed to sell this?" Angel said, turning it over, then fanning through the pages.

"That's exactly what I want to know. Where do people sell nice books? You can keep the money you get, and I'll pay you more afterward, when you tell me where you were able to sell it."

"Somebody on the streets will know what to do with it. I could just ask around."

"But if you actually sell it, you'll have the cash," Truman said. And the information would be legitimate, not some half-baked and distorted rumor from the streets.

"What do you think a book like this is worth?"

"It's used, so probably less than ten dollars."

Angel nodded. "What are you going to pay me for the information?"

"How much do you think would be fair?"

"I guess it depends on how long it takes. Let's budget for an hour to start with. How about twenty dollars?"

"I can manage that," Truman said. "But let me know if it's going to take longer."

"So I'll do it." Angel tucked the book under her arm and flashed a broad smile. "Good night, then—I've got work to do tomorrow."

With that, she walked away, turning into the alley.

"Do you trust her?" Celeste said quietly, watching her leave.

"It's just a book."

"It was a good idea to tell her you'll pay her more. She'll definitely come back."

"Biff Sturgis says that cash is the ultimate motivator. It keeps people focused."

"I get it. My *abuela* says 'With money, even the dog dances.'"

"I don't need dancing dogs," Truman said. "Just some information."

Celeste gave him an air kiss before she climbed into her car and drove off.

Upstairs, Truman got undressed and climbed into bed, and lay there gazing up at the windows, at the sky glowing with the ambient city light. It was getting warmer—he should open the middle panes in each of the windows to get some ventilation, as they were hinged for that purpose. That meant climbing up a ladder, and then more noise and grime would drift in. The building didn't have heating or air-conditioning, which meant he was either wearing sweaters and heavy socks in the cold or sitting in front of a fan in his underpants because it was too hot. But it was May, and May was still comfortable.

It was startling that the drinks at that chic wannabe speakeasy cost three times what they'd paid the night before in the anything-goes queer bar. Drinking there tonight had felt extravagant, but for somebody like Angel, both places were far out of reach. Based on the number of tents he'd seen, there were more people camped in that alley with her and Beretta than there were actually living in this building. Income inequality in this city was getting to be completely nuts.

FOUR

Celeste woke to a quiet house. Both her parents left early for their jobs, and that allowed her the luxury of solitude to enjoy her breakfast. She made toast and sliced some avocado onto it, then sprinkled it with chili flakes. After she'd cut up an orange, and savored the wedges, and rinsed her dishes, she went to get dressed for work.

Pulling out a blouse that she liked, Celeste deliberated for a moment on whether it was too low-cut to pass as office wear. What the hell, she decided. Maybe someone would drop by who would enjoy ogling her cleavage.

The illicit cash that she and Truman had acquired meant she could theoretically take a few months off, even a few years if she was careful, and spend the whole day goofing off. But she knew that too much of a good thing would quickly get boring, and she'd start to lose her connections in the art world.

The gallery was boring too, but Saffron was easy to work for, and lax about her hours and time off. In the lengthy slow periods Celeste read about artists and networked with them to keep up on their work. She had curated a couple of the recent shows at the gallery, and both had sold well, which meant she was competent in the field, at least.

Sometimes she envied Truman's freedom from being chained to a desk, and it was fun to work with him on his loopy cases, but that wasn't a career for her, poking into people's problems and dealing with lowlifes.

The gallery wasn't far from Boyle Heights, just across the river in the Arts District, and Celeste parked her little blue car in the alley out back, in one of the two spaces demarcated in yellow paint. The other space was empty, meaning Saffron wasn't here. She rarely was, being a trust-fund baby who ran the gallery mostly as a hobby and so she'd have something respectable to claim as a profession among her social set. But Saffron did know a lot about art, and more importantly knew how to sell it to rich folks, and she always made payroll.

Celeste unlocked the heavy back door and

punched the code into the alarm panel to silence the insistent beeping. The building had been converted from a factory, and the art was displayed in the large main room that had once been the factory floor. A flight of blue metal stairs led up to a mezzanine level with a set of offices, and Celeste's wide glass-topped desk sat near the front entrance.

Once she'd unlocked the door and flipped the sign in the window over to read OPEN, she settled into her desk. Scrabbling around in the drawer, she found an Ativan, and popped it in her mouth, crunching it between her teeth.

A trank, she'd heard it called, probably short for *tranquilizer*. She'd promised Truman that she'd get a handle on this stuff. One of his idiot junkie clients had noticed one evening that she was on downers, and Truman had staged a one-man intervention. So these days she cut back on it when they were hanging out. She did have a handle on it, she reminded herself. She took the stuff because she wanted to, not because she needed it. There was definitely no reason for her to be in twelve-step.

In the late morning, Truman was eating an apple and reading the news on his phone when the door buzzer sounded.

When he answered, a crackly voice said, "It's Angel."

Good thing he'd already dressed. No way did he want her coming up here, so he grabbed his keys and his wad of cash, then locked up and went down to the street. Angel was waiting for him on the sidewalk, dressed the way she had been last night, in jeans and the torn nylon jacket.

"Good morning, Sunshine."

"Why do you call me that?" Truman demanded. "Beretta said it too."

"I guess it's because you're so fresh-faced. Like a little ray of sunshine. Just out of knee pants. Not all rough and grimy and beat-down from the streets, like Beretta."

He frowned. What she was describing was a twinkie. Even though he'd never be as hard-boiled as pistol-packing Biff Sturgis, he wanted to look tough enough for this job. By the standards of the alley, though, it probably wasn't surprising that he looked soft.

"So did you sell the book?"

"I just came from there," Angel said. "It's a great big place. Books up to the ceiling. Full of people in suits reading and drinking coffee."

"So it's a bookstore? What's the name of it?"

"You've got me on that one. But it's definitely a store."

Truman stifled a sigh. "OK. Where is it?"

"That way," she said, and vaguely gestured to the west. "Outside the neighborhood. Over by a drug store."

"You walked there?"

"Sure I did. It's not far. It's kind of on a corner."

"Maybe I know the place. How did you find it?"

"I asked around," Angel said. "Someone said they buy books."

"What did they give you for it?"

"Six dollars."

Truman nodded. "Nice."

"And you owe me twenty."

Digging out his wad of cash, he found a couple of sawbucks and handed them over. "Thanks for your help."

Angel furtively surveyed the street to make sure no one had seen her pocket the cash. "Any time, Sunshine."

As he walked back up the stairs, Truman wondered if he might look tougher if he stopped using moisturizer, and let his beard grow out, and got his hair cut different. Maybe he'd take Dyson's front-desk guy up on that haircut coupon.

After he finished breakfast, he pulled on his backpack and headed out. The only bookstore in the direction Angel had pointed that was also within walking distance was just west, in the Historic Core. He'd only been in there a few times, and didn't know they bought books. That meant they sold used books. He should have thought of that place himself, but Angel had quickly found it for him, and he walked that way. Sure enough, when he came to it, it was almost on the corner, and there was a drugstore next door.

Inside he stopped for a moment to take in the space. Angel's vague description was accurate—the bookshelves went up to the ceiling, with a wheeled stepladder to access the higher shelves. There were café tables in the window where the office drones from the Financial District were making their midday escapes.

Stepping up to the information desk, Truman spoke to the red-bearded clerk. "Where can I find the UFO books?"

The guy cracked a smile. "Along the back wall, about halfway down."

"And where would I go for a biography of John Adams?"

"It's weird that you're looking for that. I just got a hardback in this morning. I haven't priced it yet."

"Can I see it anyway?"

He turned to the shelves behind him to find the volume, and handed it to Truman. Flipping open the front cover, he saw TRUMAN BOUDREAUX written in blue ink, in his own high school–era handwriting. Handing it back to the clerk, he had to smile. It meant Angel really had been here—she'd been completely straight with him.

"You seem happy to find it," the clerk said. "Give me a few minutes and I'll have a price for you."

"I'm not going to buy it," Truman said. "I'll let someone else enrich themselves reading about the man's life."

"Innocent until proven guilty," the clerk said, raising his eyebrows.

"What do you mean?"

"That was one of Adams's things. In the court system. The right to representation, and that suspects are innocent until proven guilty."

"Well, you certainly don't need to read that book."

He shrugged. "I have an MA in history."

And you're woefully underemployed, Truman thought, but didn't say that. Instead he thanked the guy and walked toward the back wall.

The UFO books were lumped into the section marked PARANORMAL, and once he was standing in front of them, he spotted *Saucers over the Southwest* almost right away. There was just one copy, with the red and white dust jacket. It really was thick, as Dyson had said. Heart pounding, Truman pulled it from the shelf and looked inside the front cover.

Under his breath, he exclaimed, *"Yes."*

The *Birth of Venus* bookplate was there. In this rendering the woman trying to throw a cloak over the goddess was cropped out. Below the image was printed "ex libris Wendy O'Connell." It was so idiosyncratic, and just the way Dyson had described it—this had to be his copy.

Penciled in the top corner of the page was "$40." That made him smile—he could definitely afford to get it back. Truman took the book to the register and handed it to the woman working there. She wore cat-eye glasses and a gray tank top over her lanky frame, and incongruously, a knitted cap.

"Forty-three eighty," she said, keying it into the register. "Are you a saucer-head?"

"Not really." Truman pulled out his cash. "But I'm interested in the field."

"This is a great resource. It has a lot of detail about the crash sites in New Mexico and Colorado, and all the cover-ups, and the sites that are here in town," she said, counting out his change.

"There are crash sites in the city? I've never heard of any."

"Not crash sites—cover-up sites. Places where people died mysteriously, or just"—she paused to spread her palms—"disappeared."

Truman frowned. "What people?"

She leaned closer and spoke intently. "People who knew too much about flying saucers."

"OK," he said evenly.

She sighed and handed him the book. "Lots of the early ufologists were Angelenos."

"I'll look forward to reading about it."

Sliding the book into his backpack, Truman went out to the street and walked back toward his loft, a smile on his face. His instinct had been right—whoever swiped the book from Dyson's desk had just wanted to make a few dollars, and there weren't a lot of places to sell books.

———•———

At his desk, he pulled out the thick volume and looked it over. Some of the pages had pink sticky-note flags attached to them, positioned to protrude just beyond the edge of the page, making them easy to find. Some of the flags had a hand-written asterisk on them, and others bore an exclamation mark or a question mark. Each of the asterisk markers was next to a street address, it seemed. Some were out of state, and some were local—in Hollywood, and La Mirada, and Colton.

But that wasn't enough. Dyson could have easily found the same material again in another copy of the book. What was so special about this one? Truman fanned through the pages, but nothing was written anywhere in the margins, and no loose notes were tucked inside. The only annotations were the sticky notes. He pulled off the dust jacket, but nothing had been written inside it either.

The cloth cover was in good shape, considering how old it was. When the book was open, he noticed, the cloth spine pulled away from the binding, which puckered inward, creating a space large enough for a finger or two. Holding the volume up to the window, he peered into the gap. There was something in there—something reflective that caught the light, near the bottom.

Setting the book face-down on his desktop, Truman aimed the flashlight on his phone into the gap, then slid off his chair, kneeling on the floor to get a better look, pulling up on the end of the spine with a fingernail. A thin black wafer was stuck to the binding with a strip of clear tape. On the little label he could make out HIGH PERFORMANCE and 128 GB. It was a mini memory card, the kind that fit in a camera or a phone.

He sat in his chair again and stared at the book. That explained why this copy was important—it wasn't about the book at all. On his phone he sent Dyson a text:

Are you at your office right now?

His reply came a moment later:

Here until six.

Truman put the dust jacket back on, then closed the book and tucked it into his backpack.

Before he left he went to his clothes rack to change pants. He knew he would never have a gym body, but Celeste said this particular pair of jeans flattered his butt.

Once he was dressed he slung on his backpack and went down to the street. The sun was inching lower in the northwest, but it would still be a while until dark. In his confident commuter gait, he walked toward Dyson's office.

A different person was on the front desk, Truman saw, once the door buzzed open and he stepped inside. She was junkie-thin, and had rough skin and sunken cheeks, with a wattle under her chin. Maybe he wouldn't stop moisturizing after all.

Looking up at him, she greeted Truman in a gravelly smoker's voice. "Can I help you?"

"I have a meeting with Dyson Norris."

She picked up the phone and spoke into it. "You have a client here to see you."

Dyson appeared a moment later, with that easy smile and wearing a billowy white shirt that showed a bit of his chest. He waved Truman back to his little office and closed the door behind them.

"Any progress?" Dyson said, and dropped into his chair.

Truman slipped off his bag and retrieved the book.

"Whoa," Dyson murmured, his eyes growing wide.

Truman handed it across the desk. When Dyson pulled open the cover, a smile spread across his face.

"You did it, man."

"I thought it looked like the right copy." Truman watched as he flipped through it, checking the sticky notes. He didn't look inside the spine.

"It is," Dyson said, looking up and beaming at him. "I thought I'd never see it again. In a city of ten million people, how did you find it?"

"That's a trade secret."

"Well, you've made me a happy man."

"And you owe me seven hundred bucks."

Dyson chuckled and reached for the canvas satchel lying at the side of his desk. Flipping it open, he dug in it for a moment, and fished out a white business envelope. Leaning over the desk, he handed it to Truman.

"You should count it," Dyson said, and leaned back in his chair.

It wasn't sealed, and Truman riffled through the C-notes, confirming that there were seven of them.

"Exact change," Truman said. "I guess you were confident that I'd find it."

"Actually, I didn't really expect that you would."

"So why did you lead with seven hundred?"

He grinned and waved a hand. "Because that's how much cash I had sitting in an envelope in my satchel."

"I see. I was also curious about why you didn't mention the memory card."

Dyson's expression shifted. He sat up and spoke quietly. "Did you look at it?"

"I didn't touch it. It's not my business. I was hired to find the book."

Dyson watched him for a moment. "I guess I believe that. How did you find the card?"

"I looked for it. I knew there had to be something unique about this copy. Your sticky notes certainly weren't irreplaceable, and you could get another one for thirty bucks."

"It's still there?"

"Of course it is," Truman said, and frowned. "Look for yourself. I said I didn't touch it. But I wondered whether I was enabling some kind of criminal enterprise."

Dyson pulled the book open and held it up to the light, peering into the gap in the spine. Satisfied, he set it on the desktop again and eyed Truman.

"You don't know what life is like down here."

"Don't put the entitled-outsider thing on me. I don't know how things are in this office, but I live twenty minutes' walk from here, so I know exactly what this neighborhood is like." He threw up his hands. "But like I said, it's none of my business what you're up to."

"I'm not a criminal," Dyson said intently. "Do you keep track of local politics?"

"I read enough to get the broad strokes."

"So you know there are plenty of crooks in local government. Deals get made behind closed doors. There's a lot of corruption."

"Sure there is. It's inevitable in a town this size, with a hundred local jurisdictions and so little journalism. Nobody's minding the store."

"I've been documenting some shady transactions between a big developer and the city," Dyson said. "Specifically concerning a plot of land right up the street, at the edge of Skid Row."

"What developer?"

"Irwin Jeffries. Have you heard of him?"

"Maybe."

"He wants to put up thirty floors of luxury condos. The project is called A Cut Above."

"Ouch."

"Right?" Dyson said emphatically, leaning on his desk. "It's not illegal, but morally it's just so wrong, and the city won't do anything to mitigate it. The city staffers are in his thrall."

"Jeffries pays them off?"

"I think that's what's happening. But how do you prove that? I'm trying to put it all together."

Truman nodded, thinking it through.

"Corruption in local government isn't really new, though, and not many people would find it surprising. Why are you hiding your evidence of it in a book?"

"If it was in my cloud drive, anyone who executed a search warrant on my phone or my computer would see what I was up to, and they could just delete it."

"Who would do that?"

He threw up his hands. "City government controls the police, and city government is where the corruption is."

Truman sighed. It sounded dubious that local politicians would go after Dyson. Lots of them had far more serious problems—several local-government agencies were subject to long-term federal oversight because of their misdeeds and incompetence, and he'd read about people at city hall who were personally embroiled in FBI investigations. But he had to admit that Dyson's story was self-consistent, even if it sounded a little paranoid.

"What are you going to do with this documentation?" Truman said.

"Jeffries promised to include transitional housing for homeless people in this project. That's how he managed to get initial approval and a big fat slew of tax breaks for it. If he goes back on his word, I'll expose all this data as evidence of the sleaze."

"Well, props for being invested in the community. I guess it's almost an extension of your job."

Dyson sat back, looking tired.

Truman shifted closer to his desk, and cleared his throat. He could feel his face warming up. "So—now that our business is concluded, would you like to go for a drink with me sometime?"

Dyson cocked his head. "Is that why you asked me if I'm a crook? So that you'd know whether you wanted to ask me on a date?"

"I guess that was part of it."

"How about right now? I'm ready to leave."

"Works for me," Truman said, and took a deep breath as he rose.

"I need to eat first, though." Dyson tucked the UFO book into his satchel and slung it on his shoulder. Eyeing Truman as he pulled open his office door, he said, "I did not see that coming. You're a sly one."

Truman chuckled. "I wanted to clear up the business stuff first."

FIVE

s they walked out together, Dyson said, "Do you know the Vietnamese diner on the corner?"

"I love that place."

Dyson waved to the receptionist as he led Truman out to the street. In a few blocks they were stepping into the diner. Truman sat across from him, with his back to the window. He already knew he wanted the *pho*, and watched Dyson as he perused the menu.

In his pants Truman's phone buzzed, and he pulled it out to check. It was a text from Celeste:

Developments? Drinks? Leaving work now.

Truman thumb-typed a reply:

Working right now.

Celeste's reply came a moment later:

I know what that means: working on a man. Is it Dyson?

Truman wrote back:

I'll call later.

Once they'd ordered, Dyson eyed him and asked, "So how did you wind up at the Gladys Park festival?"

"Angel invited us. She's kind of my neighbor—her tent is in the alley next to my building."

"I don't think I know her."

"She sang with the band—red blouse, lots of hair."

Dyson nodded. "I remember."

"She's a really talented singer. I've talked to her a few times. She seems so with it, but then there are gaps where things don't quite mesh."

"That's a good way to put it. Lots of people wind up on the streets because they can't function in specific situations."

"Are some of them there just for financial reasons? The housing shortage?"

"That's part of it," Dyson said. "It's much harder to make rent when the rent is high. But the idea that homelessness is a choice is a cruel myth."

"How many clients do you get in a week?"

"A tiny number compared to the scope of the problem. It's like trying to put out a trash fire with a glass of water. Right now there are sixty thousand people sleeping rough on any given night."

Truman waited as the waitress set down their food, then started into it.

"That woman who accused Celeste of taking her shoes," Truman said, "and the drummer who wouldn't stop drumming. It seems like there are just so many dysfunctional people."

"There are, sure, but there are all kinds of people on the streets. Dysfunctional people, and brilliant people, and addicts. But people who have nothing have a unique kind of honesty. At least when they're lucid and not trying to score. There's no bullshit, no pretense, because they're not dialed in the way you and I are." He waved his arm at the city beyond the window. "They're not slaving away to keep all this going."

"I think I can see that, in a way." He eyed Dyson for a moment. "I love that you're so passionate about it."

Dyson looked down at his plate, poking his noodles with his chopsticks. "I'm not sure it matters."

After they'd finished eating, and paid the waitress, Dyson eyed him. "You said you lived near here."

"Technically I'm in the Fashion District. It's a few minutes' walk. Do you want to come over and hang out?"

"Let's do it," he said, and grinned.

Walking toward his place, skirting the edge of Skid Row, Truman could feel a flutter in his stomach, anticipating what was going to happen next. The look in Dyson's eye had told him he understood what was implied in hanging out. The air had cooled off, and the long shadows of the end of the day consumed all but the tallest buildings, still lit in fading golden light.

From across the street, a woman shouted, "Hey, Dyson!"

Not breaking his stride, Dyson waved, and called back to her, his dialect effortlessly shifting to street: "How you doin'?"

"Friend of yours?" Truman said.

"Probably a client. I don't remember her."

In the next block, when the sidewalk narrowed along a row of tents interspersed with junk, Dyson casually put his arm around Truman's waist, guiding him past the clutter. Glancing at him, Truman had to smile at the familiarity.

At the end of the block stood a man holding a can of potato chips, absently tipping them out and munching. He gestured with the container when he caught sight of them.

"Dyson, my man."

"Hey, Tommy," he said, pausing for a moment. "How did the drugstore work out?"

"They didn't keep me there very long. You're not allowed to sample stuff."

Dyson pointed at the can. "Like potato chips?"

"Or the pharmaceuticals."

"That's too bad. You should come and see me."

"I will," he said. "You know it."

Once they were walking abreast again, Truman said, "Is Dyson a street name, or your real name?"

"It's what my mother put on my birth certificate. I think it must sound enough like a street name that nobody here tried to change it."

"Do you live in the neighborhood?"

"South Park," he said, and pointed up the street. "About two miles that way."

When they got to his building, Truman stepped up to the front door and pulled out his keys.

"I can't believe you basically live on Skid Row," Dyson said.

"It didn't used to be." Truman held the door for him to step inside. "It's the Fashion District, and all these storefronts are clothing businesses, but the tents are spreading. I see way more sleeping bags in the Historic Core these days too."

Inside Truman's loft, Dyson set his satchel on the nearest sofa and looked around.

"Great place. It's a commercial building?"

"Exactly. It's a hard lease, so the landlord provides the walls and nothing else. One of the units is an artist's live-work studio, and there's a musician in another, but I just live here."

"Did you build the bathroom?"

"Celeste's dad built it," Truman said. "I helped."

"It looks so weird with the walls ending halfway to the ceiling."

"Imagine if they went all the way up."

Dyson gazed at the white box. "You're right—that would be worse." He stepped toward the middle of the room. "You know, this would be a great place for a party. I love the sofa lounge space."

Truman stepped in front of him, and put his hands on Dyson's hips. Dyson met his mouth, intent and warm, and after a moment moved to kiss his neck. Unbuttoning his shirt, Truman ran his hands over Dyson's chest.

"You have a great body."

"Do you want to fuck me?" Dyson said, meeting his gaze.

Truman led him to the bed and let Dyson unbutton his pants. Soon they were both naked, and Truman explored his body, his warm skin, and met his mouth again, gasping as Dyson squeezed his cock.

Grabbing a condom from the bedside table,

Truman rolled it on, then moved closer. He started gently with his fingers, and eventually he was inside him. Dyson closed his eyes, breathing hard, as Truman pounded him. Wrapping an arm around his chest, Truman climaxed, shuddering, then flopped onto his side. Kissing him again, he reached for Dyson's rock-hard cock and stroked him until he came.

They lay there for a while, limbs intertwined, warm and content. Truman drifted off, waking later when Dyson got up and went into the bathroom. It was dark out now, but when he reached for his phone, he saw that it wasn't that late.

Dyson came back and climbed in with him, pulling up the covers and wrapping an arm around Truman's waist.

"It must get cold in here in winter, with the concrete and the high ceilings."

"It's impossible to stay warm," Truman said. "Right now is the only season when it's not stupid hot or freezing cold."

"The Goldilocks zone."

Truman chuckled. "Right."

"They use that term in science. It means that a planet is the right distance from a star to have liquid water, which means it's amenable to life."

"Did you read that in your flying-saucer book?"

"It's just regular science."

"I was looking at close-ups of Jupiter the

other day. The colors and the patterns are strange, but really beautiful."

"The one that freaks me out is Io," Dyson said. "I have a visceral reaction to it."

"What's Io?"

"One of the moons of Jupiter. It's covered with volcanoes. Photos of it make me nauseous."

"As my friend Celeste would say, that sounds far-fetched."

"I'll show you." Dyson pulled away and reached for his pants on the floor, returning a moment later with his phone. He tapped at it for a moment, then handed it over.

Truman studied the image on the screen. "It looks like a black-olive pizza, but they skimped on the black olives."

"And instead of cheese they used dog vomit."

"Gross," Truman said, and laughed.

"Look at it. It's disgusting. Look at that color."

"You're right, it is." He handed the phone back. "I guess not all the planets can be pretty."

"Io is a moon."

Truman shifted down the bed and adjusted the covers. "I'm kind of wiped out."

"Do you want me to go?"

"I want you to stay, if you want to."

Dyson flashed a smile and pulled him closer, notching his knees in behind Truman's.

SIX

Waking in the May-gray daylight, diffuse and gloomy from the marine layer, Truman found Dyson lying on his side, head propped on one arm, gazing at him.

"What did I miss?" Truman said. His tongue felt thick.

"Nothing." Dyson leaned in and kissed him, lingering in it. "I need to get home. I have to work today."

"You were there on Sunday too. Do you have a set schedule?"

"It's pretty irregular. I don't work every day, but I'm on for the next three."

"Anyway, I had fun," Truman said.

Dyson grinned as he climbed out of bed. "That means we should hang out again."

Truman watched him get dressed, then got up to follow him to the door, handing him his satchel and locking the deadbolt behind him.

It was early, he saw, glancing at his phone, and he climbed back into bed and slept for a while, then woke up again at a more reasonable hour.

Once he'd made coffee, he texted Celeste:

At the gallery?

Her reply was an emoji of an eye-roll, plus:

All day.

Truman got dressed and slipped his laptop into his backpack. Down on the street, he looked into the alley as he walked by, but there was no sign of life, just the tents and the shopping carts and the piles of stuff. The streets were busy, and he weaved around the pedestrians gawking in the windows of the clothing retailers, and dodged a pair of guys unloading boxes from a van parked in the curb cut.

On the other side of Skid Row was the Arts District, a similar neighborhood of erstwhile warehouse and factory buildings, but with none of the trash and grime and clusters of tents. Gentrification had shifted most of that area into tony retail and upscale apartments. The artists were long gone, but a few upscale galleries remained, like the place where Celeste worked. As he approached it, Truman admired the clean white facade, the neat planter boxes, and Saffron's name in stylishly rusted metal letters next to the door. His building had the same bones as this one but didn't look nearly as sharp. It was amazing what a little money could do.

When he stepped inside, he saw that Celeste was with a client, standing at the far wall, in front of a painting. She was wearing a black skirt and a pale-blue top that showed some cleavage.

Saffron came down the industrial-chic staircase from the offices, her heels clanking on the metal steps, moving languorously, a clutch in one hand. She looked moneyed and fashionable in a sharp linen suit, with subtle gold jewelry highlighted by her dark skin. The jacket had an odd cut, with the lapels starting just over her belt. Knowing Saffron, it was almost certainly couture.

She smiled and greeted Truman, adding quietly, "Celeste won't be long. That fellow doesn't look like a buyer."

Truman glanced at the guy. He had graying dark hair and wore a sweater and loose jeans. "How can you tell?"

"Look at his shoes. They're cheap. That painting is listed at a hundred grand."

They were hiking boots, Truman saw, which weren't necessarily inexpensive.

"That's probably a good metric," he said, "but

in LA you can never be sure."

Saffron raised her eyebrows. "Good point, detective. All those tech people on the West-side are paid obscene salaries, but they dress like they're still in middle school." She eyed the client again, then said, "I must be off. Mwah."

Truman watched as she headed toward the back door, then wandered over to look at a paint-ing near Celeste's desk, not focusing on it but rather listening to her sales pitch across the room.

"But that's how the artist defies the genre," Celeste was saying. "The lemon has three arms so that it repulses you in parallel with its oozing eroticism."

"I don't know how erotic a lemon is," the man said dubiously.

"And once again the artist has succeeded—fomenting fundamental doubt in the viewer, driving you to question things while simultane-ously transcending the banal." She paused to gaze at the painting, then folded her arms. "Look at the stippling of all that lemon flesh and tell me it's not sexually charged."

Truman watched as the guy stepped closer, peering at the canvas. From here he could see that the painting was of a distorted bright-yel-low lemon sitting among a pile of luridly colored plastic toys. One of its eyes was open, the other closed. There were two arms on one side, and it had a mouth with a creepy gummy human smile.

"I get it," the guy said finally. "What's the asking price for this piece?"

"It's a hundred, including local delivery."

"I'll have to think about it."

"Of course," Celeste said. "If I'm not here, the owner's name is Saffron. If you need multiple pieces, she might be amenable to negotiating the prices."

Celeste walked him to the front door. As he stepped out, he said, "Thanks for your insights."

Once he was gone, Truman said, "'Fomenting fundamental doubt'? The only doubt I have is why someone would paint a picture of a mutant citrus fruit."

"Don't be making fun of my spin," she said, walking to her desk. "Else I'll have to foment you upside the head."

Truman chuckled at that, and sat in the chair across the desk from her.

"You're right, though. *Lemon Study 4* is a tough sell."

"Is that guy going to buy it?"

"Fifty-fifty. He seems really into it, but it's not cheap."

"Saffron thinks he doesn't have any money."

"She's wrong," Celeste said. "He told me he just bought an office building, and he needs art for the lobby that will impress his clients."

"The advantage of that piece is that it will impress them in addition to fomenting their fundamental doubt."

"Such an art skeptic. I'm glad you're not a buyer. That artist is very hot right now." She leaned back in her chair and crossed her knees. "So you slept with Dyson."

"I found his book for him, so I figured he wasn't a client anymore."

"Where was his book?"

Truman told her about Angel's report on the bookstore, and finding the memory card, and Dyson's explanation for it.

"I know about that guy Jeffries," Celeste said. "He's definitely a trash bag. He gets tax exemptions to build luxury condos for Chinese investors. They sit empty fifty weeks of the year while the owners are home in Shanghai, and forty thousand people are sleeping on the streets."

"Sixty thousand, according to Dyson."

"I believe it. They're everywhere. Saffron pays a company to keep them out of our alley."

"That's crazy," Truman said. "The money she spends on keeping them away should go into solving the problem."

"That would involve serious systemic changes, like tax policy and zoning laws. It's way above my pay grade, and Saffron's." She sighed. "At least the company that keeps the alley clear hires homeless people to deal with the other homeless people."

"I wonder if they went through Dyson's office."

Celeste furrowed her brow. "You know, I would think that any dealings a developer like Jeffries has with city planning would be public record."

"Dyson said there are clandestine meetings. That's the evidence he put on the memory card. If it were publicly available, he wouldn't have to hide it."

"So what has he got? Did he wiretap them?"

"Maybe he got documentation from some insider at Jeffries's company, or at city hall."

"Does it feel like that to you?" Celeste said. "He put it on a memory card. Why not use online storage like everyone else?"

"He said he didn't want it deleted if he got searched."

"If it were me, I'd just share it with other people. They can't delete every copy."

Truman nodded. "That bothered me too. It must be something that only Dyson has."

"But why put it on a memory card? It doesn't sound like evidence—more like blackmail material."

"Dyson isn't that guy."

"See, this is what happens when you sleep with someone. You lose all objectivity."

Truman shrugged. "At this point, it doesn't really matter. I did what he paid me to do."

"If he's blackmailing Irwin Jeffries, he's putting himself in danger. That guy is ruthless."

"I suspect Dyson can take care of himself."

"Still, wouldn't you love to know what was on that memory card?"

"I was tempted to look at it, but that would have been unethical."

Her eyes narrowed. "Maybe you're too ethical."

Truman chuckled. "I'll ask him for details when I see him again."

"So Dyson is a repeat."

"We talked about it, yeah."

"Well, tell him he's out of his league if he's trying to chisel Irwin Jeffries."

<hr>

Truman left the gallery a while later and walked toward the central library, avoiding the roughest part of Skid Row by taking the streets through Little Tokyo. Celeste had good instincts, he knew that, and she was probably more objective about Dyson than he was.

At the library he found a space at one of the big heavy tables in the ESL room. He never made use of the materials in here, but he loved the vibe, the heavy furniture and the pillars and the murals, century-old depictions of the Crusades. The dark colors and painted greenery felt cozy and enveloping, which helped him focus, a yin counterpoint to the yang of the daylight and the frenetic city outside.

Pulling open his computer, he started reading about Irwin Jeffries and the condo project he was developing on Skid Row. There had been some media coverage of A Cut Above, and a lot had been written by an anti-gentrification group, who described the project much the way Dyson had. The city's description of the plan was predictably light on details but said that the complex would include transitional housing.

Elsewhere, one of the critics went into more depth, explaining that the original compromise with the city bureaucracy on transitional housing was to have separate entrances, so that the wealthy and the poor wouldn't cross paths. Apparently some politicians had balked at how that might be perceived by voters, and the next offer from Jeffries was to build two separate buildings, A Cut Above and a smaller building, with affordable housing rather than transitional housing, called Under Cut. From what Truman could find, that seemed to be the final configuration.

There had to be more to what Dyson was up to. Nothing he'd read implied that any evidence he had about the project could be so explosive that the city would send the cops after him or subpoena his digital files. Celeste's surmise seemed more plausible now, and if she was right—that he was trying to extort Jeffries—Dyson really was in danger.

Explaining that to Dyson was pointless, but maybe he could find out what exactly he was holding, what was so sensitive that it couldn't inhabit the cloud. He could use the pretext of their intimacy to ask. Truman sat back and gazed absently up at the painted Crusaders. If he was honest with himself, was that his only motivation? He did want to get to know Dyson better, so any concern he had about extortion was intertwined with that. He could at least ask Dyson about it, he decided. The worst thing that could happen is that he pushed back.

Pulling out his phone, he sent Dyson a text:

Do you have time to get together today?

On his computer again, he read more about Jeffries's past projects. The developer was responsible for some of those fuggly sterile towers lumped around that stupid stadium. In an article dated a few years ago, a journalist had tried to parse his intricate connections to several local city governments. Part of the game appeared to be that Jeffries donated heavily to charities controlled by politicians, and unlike direct political contributions, there was no limit to how much he could give to a fund that was registered as a charity. The journalist outlined how Jeffries had sunk a hundred grand into an art charity controlled by a politician's wife, and showed that the group wasn't particularly charitable, having disbursed less than four grand in over a decade.

Enough, he decided, wrinkling his nose and folding his computer closed. There was so much freaking sleaze. Dyson hadn't responded yet, he saw, glancing at his phone. The gallery would be closing soon, so he texted Celeste:

Still at work?

Her reply came a moment later:

Barely. Planning to go home and put on my PJs.

Truman wrote back:

Right away? I need a drink.

Before long, her answer came, and it made him smile:

How about that pub at Union Station?

Truman packed up his computer and walked out to the lobby, then to the street, and around the corner to the metro. A couple of stops later, he was climbing up out of the ground at Union Station.

The classic pub, across the courtyard from

the station, had a fun 1940s vibe and a clientele that was usually a pleasant mix of commuters and out-of-towners. It wasn't busy at this hour, and Truman made his way to the bar.

"A blended margarita," he told the bartender when he came over.

When his drink arrived, as Truman was digging in his pants for cash, Celeste came in and perched on the stool beside him.

"Bring me a small of a pilsner or a pale lager," she told the bartender.

The guy stared at her with a blank expression. "I don't think we have that."

"Then a small of whatever is the wateriest beer on tap."

He nodded and plucked Truman's twenty before he stepped away.

"So I did some research," Truman said, and told her what he'd read about Jeffries's history, and the two-building solution at the condo project to keep the low-income housing away from the upmarket units.

Celeste paused to pay the bartender, then clinked her glass against Truman's. "So the city is down with two buildings, but not with two entrances?"

"Everyone with a say in it seems to be on board with the new plan," he said. "The city has definitely signed off on it."

"No matter how it's enacted, it's economic apartheid."

"One of the homeless advocates used that word too," Truman said. "They're the big dissenting voice, but they're basically powerless. At the public meetings the activists were treated like gadflies—either not allowed to speak or time-limited to a few minutes. One writer said the officials changed the date and venue of the meeting at the last minute so that fewer people would show up."

"It's so corrupt."

"The only place in the country where it's worse is Chicago, apparently."

She waved an arm. "How can anyone know that? How do you empirically measure sleaze?"

"Someone tried, at least. One of the stories was about a Jeffries subcontractor. He built an extension onto a house owned by the mother-in-law of a city employee. It's hard to prove it was a bribe, but why else would he do a hundred and fifty grand worth of work for free?"

"That's totally a bribe," she said, and sipped her beer.

"It makes me think that Dyson has that kind of evidence. Like you said, maybe he's going to extort the guy."

"Have you talked to him?"

"I tried, but he kind of ghosted me."

"You don't have to leave it at that. You still

have a business relationship."

"You're right." Truman sighed. "I need to track him down."

When she'd finished her beer, Celeste looked around the bar. "It's mostly out-of-town type guys."

"We can just go."

Celeste stood up and smoothed the front of her skirt. "My car is in the lot under the station. I'll give you a ride."

They walked through the long concourse under the tracks, then down the stairs to the parking lot.

———◆———

As she pulled up to his building, Truman said, "Are you at the gallery tomorrow?"

"All day. Let me know how it goes with Dyson."

After he climbed out, Celeste navigated to Boyle Heights in the deepening twilight, turning onto her quiet street and parking in the driveway behind Ernesto's truck. Inside, he was stretched out in his recliner, fast asleep. The slack expression on his face made her smile. Her mother, María, was on the sofa, wearing a dark sweater, her long hair pulled back. She paused the TV program she was watching.

"You went out after work?" she asked.

"I just needed to catch up with Truman."

"You need to meet some straight boys."

Celeste chuckled. "That's actually the last thing I need. What are you watching?"

"A documentary about the civil rights era."

"Doesn't that get you steamed? All the injustice?"

"Just the opposite. It reinforces how much has changed for the better, and reminds me that most people don't want it to be 1957 again."

"I hope that's true."

"Sit down," María said, and patted the cushion beside her.

Celeste joined her, partly tuned in to the television and María's running commentary, and partly reading on her phone. Eventually she kissed María good night and went to her room.

Climbing into bed, with the lights out, she thought about the day. Truman really was wide-eyed sometimes, and he was being a little naive about Dyson. But she had her own stuff to worry about, like making some sales in the current exhibition so that she could get something fresh in there. Enough pieces sold that Saffron was happy to let her curate, and it wasn't even on Celeste's head if they didn't, because the two of them usually collaborated on choosing the pieces. But if the art sat there for too long, it got as stale as old bread.

SEVEN

In the morning, Truman shivered as he crossed the cold floor to the espresso maker. Climbing back into the comfort of his bed with a steaming cup, he checked his phone—still no response from Dyson. The guy had said he wanted to get together again, and at this point it was just plain rude not to write back. Thinking about it, Dyson said he'd be working today, and he knew where that was.

First he spent some time reading the news, then made another espresso before he got dressed, choosing a pair of light cotton pants for the warm day that was predicted.

The marine layer had already burned off and the sun was bright, he found, stepping outside onto the street. The alley looked quiet, and turning the corner, he walked past a strip of three *quinceañera* shops. He could never figure out why they were all right there, side-by-side, when they sold the same kind of stuff—sparkly party dresses for the fifteen-year-old girls who were coming out and sleek tuxes for their boy companions. Maybe it was like gas stations: some intersections had one on every corner.

Truman walked past Dyson's office, farther into the Historic Core to Broadway, where he went into the vegan doughnut store and bought a doughnut for breakfast. It was more like lunchtime now, he had to concede, munching on it as he walked back toward Skid Row. Dropping the empty wrapper in a trash bin, he wiped his mouth and stepped into Dyson's office.

Mike, the anxious guy who was afraid of electricity, was on the front desk.

"I remember you," Mike said, looking up at him. "You're here for Dyson?"

"That's right."

"He's not in today."

Truman frowned. "Are you sure? He told me he was working."

"We thought he was too. Carol is handling his clients. Let me call her."

"I'm not actually—"

Mike held up a finger to silence him as he peered at the desk phone. He jabbed at the buttons, and Truman could hear it ring through the tinny speaker. Truman had to smile—since last time, he'd obviously figured out how to use the phone without picking up the receiver. A woman's voice answered.

"One of Dyson's clients is here," Mike said loudly, leaning toward the device.

"I'll be right out," she said.

Mike looked up at Truman. "She'll be right out."

"Great."

His brow furrowed. "I still have some of those haircut coupons."

"Are they for a barbershop?"

"It's a cosmology school."

"You mean a cosmetology school."

His eyes narrowed. "That's what I said. They'll cut it for free for practice, but there's no guarantee of the outcome. I think you have to sign a liability waiver."

A woman appeared from the hallway. In her fifties, she had dried-out red hair that was pulled back in a bundle, and wore jeans and a pilled sweater, the sleeves rolled up. She looked ready to paint an apartment or help someone move.

"I'm Carol," she said, and smiled. "Come on back."

Her office was similar to Dyson's in its limited square footage and in the piles of paperwork cluttering her desk.

"Have a seat," she said, stepping in and leaving the door open. "So—has Dyson got you some interviews? We can definitely help you get some better clothes. What's your name?"

"Truman, and I'm not a client," he said, and frowned. "I'm a friend of Dyson's. I thought he was working today."

She leaned back in her chair. "So did I. He left a message on the office machine that he was taking a few personal days."

"Does he often do that?" Truman said. "Take time off on short notice?"

"Never. It's weird." She eyed him for a moment. "So he's your friend? When did you last talk to him?"

Truman thought about it. "Yesterday morning."

"I've called his cell twice today—I wanted him to fill me in on a couple of clients—but he's not answering."

From the lobby came the sound of rising voices.

"There's only one counselor today, and she's with a client," Mike said.

"I don't need a counselor," a woman's voice said sharply. "I need to talk to your supervisor."

"You'll have to excuse me," Carol said, and stood up. "It sounds like someone's having an episode."

Truman followed her out to the lobby. The woman standing in front of Mike's desk looked upset, but she wasn't homeless—she wore a sharp charcoal suit and simple gold jewelry. Her hair was pulled back in tidy cornrows, and he knew that those took time and money. She looked up at Carol, then at Truman.

"Is one of you the boss?"

"That's me today," Carol said.

"Did you hear from Dyson? I can't get hold of him."

"And you are?"

"His sister."

"Ivy, isn't it?"

She nodded, calmer now. "That's me."

"I'm Carol. I do the same job as Dyson. He was scheduled to be here this morning, but he left a message last night that he was taking a few personal days. I tried to phone him, but it went straight to voice mail."

"What time did he call?"

"Around 7:40. After the office was closed."

"He left me the same message," Ivy said. "But it makes no sense."

"I don't know what to tell you," Carol said, putting her hands on her hips. "That's all I know."

"Did he have any meetings scheduled for out of the office? Maybe he was taking a client to an interview, or to buy clothes, or a training session somewhere."

Carol slowly shook her head. "That kind of stuff would be on the books, but there's nothing like that."

"Can you ask around? Maybe one of your clients talked to him." Ivy reached into her jacket and produced a business card, then stepped toward Carol and handed it to her.

"I'll do that. If the streets know anything, I'm sure I'll hear about it."

Ivy thanked her and turned to leave, stepping out to the street.

"I have to go," Truman said, and hustled out the door after her, trotting to catch up. "Ivy—hold up," he called.

She stopped and turned back.

"My name is Truman," he said. "I'm a friend of Dyson's."

"I've never heard him talk about you," she said, her brow furrowing.

"We just met on Sunday."

Ivy gave him the once-over. "Are you sure you're not a client?"

"We went out for dinner Monday night."

"Like a date?"

"Exactly."

"I don't know what to believe. You could be anybody."

"We talked about science," Truman said. "Dyson told me about Io, and how it freaks him out."

Her expression softened. "Io does freak him out. Do you know anything about where he might be today?"

"No—but do you have a minute to grab a coffee?"

"As long as it's on the way to the library," Ivy said.

Truman gestured up the block. "There's a place on Fifth."

As they walked abreast through the Historic Core, Truman said, "Do you work at the library?"

"Correct. I handle the special collections."

"How are they special?"

"It just means everything that's not books— maps, photographs, posters."

"I go there all the time," Truman said. "I was in there yesterday. I love the ESL room."

"I don't work directly with the public."

"So Dyson's phone is turned off?"

"I think so. That's why it goes directly to voice mail. I must have left him a dozen messages by now."

"When did he call you?"

"Around the same time Carol mentioned— like 7:30 last night. I haven't been able to reach him since."

"He's never done anything like this before?"

"It's completely out of character."

"Dyson said he lived in South Park. Have you been to his place?"

"I spoke to his roommate today. The guy never leaves the apartment. He says Dyson hasn't been home since yesterday morning."

"That's the last time I saw him too."

Ivy eyed him and frowned. "Where?"

"He was on his way to his apartment from my place. It was early."

"I guess that indicates what kind of date it was."

Ivy pulled open the door to the coffeehouse, and Truman followed her inside.

"Just get me a soy latte," she said, and went to a table by the window.

Truman stepped up to the counter and ordered, then glanced at Ivy as he waited for the drinks to come up. She really did look worried, frowning as she gazed absently out at the street.

Once he had the coffee cups in hand, he took them over and sat across from her.

"How much was it?" Ivy said.

"Forget it."

Ivy murmured thanks and sipped at the foam.

"Before they built the Music Center, this corner was the philharmonic auditorium. They used to run movies and boxing matches here too. It finally got torn down in 1985."

Her brow furrowed. "It sounds like you really have been hanging around the library."

"I used to be a tour guide."

"Where did you meet Dyson?"

"At a festival on Skid Row. And I'm not homeless, so don't ask."

Ivy chuckled at that and sipped her coffee.

"I'm a detective. Dyson hired me to find something that he'd lost."

Her eyebrows shot up. "You're a detective?"

"I don't carry a gun or have facial scars," Truman said, scowling at her, "but I'm damn good at it. I recovered what he had stolen from him."

Ivy showed her palms. "Fine with me. I don't know you."

"What do you know about Dyson's involvement with Irwin Jeffries?"

Her expression shifted. "Do you think Jeffries got to him?"

"What does Dyson have on that guy?"

"He didn't tell you? How do you know about Jeffries?"

"Dyson asked me to track down a memory card. He told me it was his stash of documents about Jeffries's luxury tower on Skid Row."

"So you had the memory card."

"For a short time. I didn't actually look at what was on it."

"An honorable man," Ivy said, eyeing him. "What planet are you from?"

"Not Io," Truman said flatly.

He knew the look in Ivy's eye, and he hated it. She called him "honorable" as if it were a synonym for "stupid." It wasn't about being honorable—it was about being loyal. Biff Sturgis said a hard-nosed detective's loyalty was always to the client, and quoted an old song: "I'll dance with the one that brung me." He meant that you didn't switch allegiance just because someone else offered to pay you more. But if Ivy thought Truman was stupid, she was underestimating him—and that might give him an advantage.

"Was Dyson lying to me?" he demanded. "What was on that memory card?"

"Normally I'd say it was none of your business. But I'm worried that Dyson has already made his play, and it seems like you're already involved."

"What play?"

Ivy looked down at her cup. "Dyson had some dirt on Jeffries."

"About the Skid Row project?"

She waved absently. "Whenever he gets that kind of information, he shares it with all his Skid Row activist homies. Strength in numbers, he says. What was on that card was different—it was about Jeffries personally."

Truman waited as she cradled her cup and

shifted in her chair.

"Dyson had photos of Jeffries at a white supremacist rally in the 1980s."

"Gross."

Ivy nodded. "Agreed."

"Is he the only one who has these photos? Where did he get them?"

She looked toward the window for a moment, at the pedestrians moving past, before she spoke. "Dyson was so steamed about this A Cut Above thing that he started to dig deeper. People have accused Jeffries of a lot over the years, but nothing ever sticks. Dyson decided to go to the little town in Oregon where the guy grew up. He hung out there for a few days. A research vacation, he called it. He scoured the public library and the town archives for material on Jeffries. On the Saturday, he went to an estate sale and found a bunch of old negatives."

"You mean photo negatives?"

"Right. The seller said that his father, the guy who had died, used to photograph all the events in this little town as a hobby. Sometimes he sold images to newspapers if it was something newsworthy. Dyson had the feeling that there might be something about Jeffries among them."

"The seller didn't recognize Jeffries in the photos?" Truman said, and sipped his espresso.

"No one knew what was in them. Before

digital photography, people shot slide film or negative film. Slide film was expensive, and printing photos from negatives was expensive. The most economical way was to shoot negative film but not print everything. You can't really tell what's in an image by looking at the negative, so they would make contact sheets. The positive image was the same size as the negative, and a whole bunch of them were printed together on a sheet of photo paper. Then if the positive version looked interesting under a magnifying glass, you could make a larger print."

"Is that knowledge you've gleaned from your job?"

Ivy ginned. "I've worked with similar materials—historical image collections. Anyway, the box that Dyson found contained only negatives, no prints or contact sheets, so no one knew what was in them. The seller assumed it was old photos of the Fourth of July parades and beauty pageants and high school football. Dyson bought everything for a few hundred dollars. The seller thought he was crazy. 'I was probably the first black guy he'd ever met,' Dyson said."

Truman nodded. "Oregon is super white."

"Dyson had no idea what he'd find. He hauled it all back to LA and spent months scanning in every strip of negative and poring over the images."

"He didn't have to make contact sheets?"

"You can convert a negative into a regular photo with a scanner and image-processing software."

"So he found pictures of Jeffries," Truman said. "What did they show, exactly?"

"Jeffries and his friends at a full-on neo-Nazi march. Torches and flags and brown shirts."

"They were color negatives?"

"Not the whole collection, but the ones of Jeffries were."

"What did he do with the images?"

"I know he isolated them on a memory card," Ivy said. "It has to be the one he asked you to find. How did he misplace it?"

"It was inside a book that got swiped from his desk," he said, gesturing with a hand. "One of his clients took the book to make some quick cash. Whoever sold it wasn't aware that the memory card was in it."

"How did you get it back?"

"That's not important. I handed the book to Dyson Monday afternoon, with the memory card still inside it. What was the play you were afraid he had made?"

"Dyson was talking about selling the photos to Jeffries."

Celeste's suspicions had been right, he thought, eyeing Ivy. And Ivy's explanation fit better than what Dyson had told him.

"Did they meet?" Truman said.

"I don't know—I told him not to do it, that it was dangerous. Like poking a wasps' nest with a stick. After that he stopped sharing his plans with me."

Truman drained his little cup and thought for a minute. "So what Dyson was really selling was his silence about the photos. Blackmail."

"Stupid, right?"

"I wonder, though—how damaging would it really be? The white-supremacist thing isn't that far-out these days. In DC it could get you a political appointment with a fat salary."

"This isn't DC," Ivy said flatly. "It would tank any goodwill that Jeffries has in this town, and damage his brand."

"I guess that makes sense."

"It's not just everyday racism, Truman. They were carrying German swastika flags."

"I get it. It's extreme."

"Besides, Jeffries isn't completely autonomous. He has shareholders, and they have a say in what his company does."

"So you think it would be a scandal if the photos got distributed."

"It would cause serious damage," Ivy said. "I'd bet his board would make him step aside to protect their assets."

Truman nodded. "So we don't know whether Dyson met Jeffries or not. Do you have any way to track his car, or his phone?"

"He drives a beater, so there's no high-tech connection to any network. I thought maybe the cops could check their plate-reader records, or find out where his phone was, so I went to talk to them this morning."

"Did you tell them about Jeffries and the photos?"

"Not that part." She looked down and cradled her cup. "I didn't want to implicate Dyson in a felony. I just said that he was missing."

"Did they look for his car, or try to trace his phone?"

"They won't do it. I shouldn't have told them that he left me that message. They said that if Dyson told me he'd be back in a few days, they have to wait a few days before they can act."

"I don't have to wait a few days," Truman said.

"You're going to look for him?" She threw up her hands. "Where?"

"Maybe I'll ask Jeffries if they spoke."

"He's an important man," Ivy said. "It might be difficult to get face time."

"Do you have a photo of Dyson?"

"I'll text it to you."

She pulled out her phone, and Truman recited his number. The photo came a moment later. Looking at it on his screen, he saw that it was a head shot of Dyson, smiling and looking into the camera. His hair was different—shorter, maybe—but otherwise he looked the same.

"I have to get to work." Ivy rose, and meeting his eye, said, "Thank you."

"I haven't done anything yet," Truman said.

"Thank you for taking me seriously."

EIGHT

After she left, he ordered another espresso and sipped it while he watched the traffic outside the window, thinking through everything Ivy had told him. Jeffries had to have an office somewhere, and he soon found it on his phone. It was close to here, in the Financial District. Truman slammed the rest of his coffee and headed out.

A few blocks' walk brought him to the address for Jeffries's company, which turned out to be an office tower. Strolling into the lobby, he approached the security guard, a burly guy with a shaved head.

"What floor is Irwin Jeffries's company on?"

The guard looked him over. "Do you have an appointment?"

The monitor in front of this guy had a grid of camera feeds, Truman saw, and there had to be dozens of tenants in this building. His job was to keep the riffraff out, not to handle appointments.

"I have a meeting with some of Jeffries's people. It's due to start right about now. Do you need to see my ID?" Truman raised his eyebrows. "I can call up there if you want someone to verify."

The guy looked away. "Floor forty-two."

"Thank you," Truman said, and stepped toward the elevators. He hated to use his white privilege that way, acting impatient and inconvenienced. But it had got him through the door.

He rode up alone in the car, and stepped out to find that forty-two had only one tenant. A wall of blond wood bore sleek brushed-metal letters that read JEFFRIES, mounted at eye level. Next to them was a set of double doors in the same luxe finish. Truman pushed his way inside to find a chic carpeted room with a reception desk made of the blond wood. Corridors led in opposite directions at either side. A pale woman was seated at the desk, wearing a somber suit jacket, her blond hair swept into an updo. Heavy makeup obfuscated her real age, probably around fifty. This was the real gatekeeper, he knew.

The receptionist looked up at him. "Can I help you?"

"I'd like to see Irwin Jeffries."

She suppressed a smile. "Mr. Jeffries is not in today."

Truman could feel his face heating up, reacting to her smug condescension. "Maybe I can talk to one of his staff?"

"What is this regarding?"

"Jeffries has been implicated in a missing-person case. If you want to stonewall me, I can have him subpoenaed for a deposition," Truman said, waving his arm at the room, "but it might be easier if I could just talk to someone here."

She raised her eyebrows. "It sounds like you should get in touch with the legal department."

"Are you sure you don't want to run this by someone with more authority than the person watching the front door?"

Scowling, she picked up the phone and murmured into it. A moment later a woman stepped out of the corridor on the right, wearing a gray suit, her wavy black hair bundled behind her head. Through her dark-rimmed glasses, she gave him an impatient once-over.

"What can I help you with?"

"Who are you, exactly?"

She frowned. "Martina. I'm Irwin's assistant."

"Truman," he said, and stepped closer. "I have some questions about Irwin's whereabouts this week."

"Are you a cop?"

"A private investigator." That wasn't true, as he didn't have a PI license, but he'd already blustered his way this far.

"I'm not going to answer any questions like that," Martina said.

Truman noticed the pin on her lapel, an enameled cartoon eye with spiky eyelashes. He'd seen it before—why did he know that little doodle?

"What dealings have you had with Dyson Norris?" Truman said, putting his hands on his hips.

"I don't know that name."

"Are you sure about that?" He watched her reaction closely, but she showed no sign of recognition.

"Mr. Truman," she said firmly, "you'll have to go. I can't help you."

"Can I set up an appointment to talk to Jeffries?"

"If you're investigating a legal matter, you can talk to his personal attorney. Would you like me to get you the name of the firm?"

"Don't bother," Truman said, and turned to leave. Walking out, he ignored the smirking gaze of the receptionist. He hated that passive-aggressive type.

Idiot, he told himself on the ride down. What had he been thinking? Of course they weren't just going to usher him into Jeffries's office and serve him biscotti. By going in there, and introducing himself, and running his mouth, he'd shown his hand, and for no payoff. Biff Sturgis would be very disappointed. He needed to strategize—acting rash like this was worse than pointless.

Walking the streets of downtown toward his place, he thought it through. Maybe it hadn't been a totally useless visit. That lapel pin—he remembered now where he'd seen it. They'd given those out at a women's event at a little bar right back there in the Financial District. Celeste had got one too. Neither of them drank there very often, but Celeste would remember the pin.

Once he was home, Truman ate an apple and a nutty granola bar, then stretched out on the sofa with an Italian soda and his copy of *Eleven Steps to Becoming a Hard-Nosed Detective*. Biff didn't have all the answers, but reading him usually helped Truman think more clearly.

In the index he looked up "blackmail." The relevant passage was several pages that mostly talked about how to detect it, with a cautionary addendum:

> If you've got the goods on someone, don't succumb
> to temptation, brother, no matter how tantalizing
> the payoff. Even a milquetoast patsy might be
> desperate enough to respond by delivering the
> blackmailer's ultimate reward—and that involves
> you on a slab in the morgue.

Truman considered what he'd learned about Dyson from Ivy. Not everything Dyson had told him was a lie, but a lot of it was. Jeffries might have reacted badly to a blackmail attempt, which could explain his disappearance. But then why had Dyson left those messages?

A plan was starting to coalesce in his mind. He found the section in Biff's book titled "Flipping a Chump." When he'd first seen that heading, he had assumed it was about some fighting technique, as Biff talked a lot about fisticuffs, being all 1930s and hard-boiled, and about carrying a gun, which he referred to as "packing a heater." Truman never intended to do that, but flipping a chump was more useful—it was Biff's explanation of the benefits of convincing someone to work with you:

> The average sap in this world is trying to keep his head down, taking care of what he's got before someone bigger comes along and takes it away. That means there are plenty of opportunities to win him over—the carrot rather than the stick. The right amount of cash, a mutual favor, even cajoling him to do his patriotic duty can flip a chump to your cause. With a dame, you have the added option to make love to her, to melt her heart and get her to see things your way. So palm a fin and slip it to that bellboy, take that steno girl to a dancehall, or loan your jalopy to that basement-dwelling janitor for the weekend—you'll soon have a firm ally in your research.

Almost a century later, it still rang true, although "making love" must have meant something more like flirting, or hitting on people, and Truman certainly wasn't limited to flirting only with the dames.

Thinking about it, the event organizer that night wouldn't give him an eye-doodle pin because it was women's night, so maybe Martina was a woman's woman. With any luck, that cozy little bar was her regular hangout.

First, Truman sent a text to Ivy:

You were right: Jeffries is difficult to get to. I'm following another lead. More tomorrow.

Next he texted Celeste:

Can I drop by the gallery?

Her response came soon after:

Super busy up in here, but I might have a moment for you.

That made him grin. Passersby rarely walked in to Saffron's gallery, and when they did, they didn't linger. But big-dollar sales didn't require lots of bodies—just a few rich ones.

Outside it was still broad daylight, but the workday in the neighborhood was winding down, and some of the businesses were already shuttered. Adopting his rapid gait, Truman headed for the Arts District.

NINE

In the gallery, Celeste had put dance music on the sound system and cranked it up. She'd been alone most of the day, except when Saffron had popped in to make some phone calls. Celeste had talked to a couple of artists, and reached out to that potential buyer for *Lemon Study 4*. She was sick of looking at the piece—it would be nice to get it off the wall. But right now she needed a nonchemical pick-me-up, and that was upbeat music.

Truman stepped in and beamed at her, raising his voice over the music. "Get down," he said, and danced over to her desk, stepping sideways and snapping his fingers.

As she looked to her computer to lower the volume, Celeste had to grin. Upbeat, unsinkable

Truman. He was a whole other kind of pick-me-up.

"Are you on your own?" he said, and dropped into the chair across from her, setting his backpack on the floor.

"As always. You're in a good mood."

"I shouldn't be. I went to see Dyson today, and he's gone missing."

Celeste frowned. "Are you kidding me?"

"You were right about what was on that memory card." He told her about the phone messages Dyson had left, and meeting Ivy, and visiting Jeffries's office. "It was stupid of me just to walk in there. I should have had a plan."

"So did Ivy ask you to look for Dyson?"

"Not directly, but I figure he was my client. I have a vested interest."

"Plus you want to sleep with him again."

"It's more than that," Truman said. "I'm worried that Jeffries might have murdered him and buried his body out in the Mojave."

"Before you started doing detective work, I would have said that sounded far-fetched."

Truman just pursed his lips and nodded. On his last case, the pair of them had stopped someone from doing precisely that.

"What an idiot." Celeste pushed her hair back, then gestured emphatically with both hands. "Dyson is an idiot if he got himself killed."

"He left those messages, though. It makes me

think something else is going on."

"Maybe Jeffries coerced him into making those calls so that no one would look for him."

"If that's the case, it worked perfectly," Truman said. "The cops won't touch it."

"If you can't get to Jeffries, what's your next angle?"

"That involves you, and hanging out in a bar."

Celeste chuckled. "Right on."

Truman told her about Jeffries's assistant, Martina, and how she had been wearing the cartoon eye pin from the event they'd also been at.

"Biff Sturgis says that most people are predisposed to being won over. It just takes the right carrot—cash, or a favor, or romance. If we can track down Martina at that bar, we could offer her one of those."

"You and that book," Celeste said. "I do remember those pins—it was some kind of lesbian event."

"So if Martina is still wearing it, maybe she's a woman's woman."

"That doesn't seem like a great indicator for sexual orientation. I was dancing with all those women too. What does she look like?"

"Gray suit, glasses, Latin—a little darker than you. Her hair is kind of wild and wiry, and she had it pulled back in a bundle, with zero product in it."

Celeste nodded. "That means she's totally gay."

"So let's use that," Truman said, and chuckled.

"Meaning I should flirt with her."

"Exactly. Wear a low-cut top and do your makeup all glam."

"That works with guys," Celeste said. "To appeal to a woman is a whole other ball game."

"So you'll wear a flannel shirt and hiking boots."

"That won't do it either. You know, there's no guarantee she'll be there. If she's not a barfly, more than likely she won't be."

"Then we'll sit there and get hammered and come up with plan B."

"What if she's straight?" Celeste said. "You have to dress up a little too. We can present the irresistible dichotomy."

"I don't think that'll work. Martina already knows me, and knows what I want."

"Still, wear something decent. That shirt with the brown and gold circles."

"You think?" Truman frowned. "It's kind of disco."

"You're kind of disco," she said pointedly.

Truman threw up his hands. "It would be pointless to deny that."

"This'll be fun. I'll have to put some work into my outfit."

Truman got up and slung on his bag.

"What time should we hit the place?" Celeste said.

"Presumably Martina works until six, and that bar is right around the corner from Jeffries's office. She might go there after work."

"So we'll go early. Should I pick you up?"

"I can walk. Text me when you're heading over." He stepped toward the door. "And wear that pin."

After he was gone, Celeste checked the clock. She might as well close up now, as she'd need time to get dressed. She killed the music altogether and then locked the front door, flipped the sign over to say CLOSED, and set the alarm. In the alley, she climbed into her little blue car, and headed across the river toward home.

The house was quiet when she got in. It was early—her parents would still be at their jobs. Digging through her closet, looking at tops and pants, she mulled what might attract the attention of a woman who hung out at that little bar. The place was dark and cozy, and it wasn't a dive, so dressing grungy was out. It wasn't a scene either, so Martina didn't go there for trends and labels and people-watching. Celeste had to wear something unique.

Eventually she settled on a sheer white shirt with a wide pointy collar and cuffed sleeves. It looked like a dress shirt, except it was cut to accommodate her breasts, and was meant to be worn mostly unbuttoned. A black bra, she decided, rather than the red. The pants she chose were gray with a subtle plaid pattern in the fabric.

Carrying a bag didn't seem quite right, so she tucked her cash and phone and ID into her pants pockets. The pin, she remembered. Digging in her jewelry box, sure enough, she'd kept it. A little drawing of an eye with big lashes, transcribed into metal. Not on the shoulder, she decided, holding it up in the mirror. It was too small. It looked better attached to the collar.

Once she'd styled her hair to look windblown and unkempt, she went out to her car and drove back downtown. The evening parking rates at the surface lots were extortionate, so she drove around for a few minutes, eventually finding a street space not far from the bar. Before she climbed out, she sent Truman a quick text:

Almost there.

This part of the Financial District was mostly sterile after office hours, the streets tidy and quiet. When Celeste strolled into the little bar, however, it was already busy. She stood for a moment to survey the crowd, letting her eyes adjust to the low lighting. Most of the stools at the bar were occupied. The rest of the room was a quartet of neat sofas and some lounge chairs arranged in tight formation. The surrounding decor was book-shelves lined with old hardbacks. She hadn't put it together before, but this place was only a couple of blocks from the central library. Maybe the intention was to echo the design of that grand building.

Three of the sofas had people on them, dressed like they had come directly from their office jobs. A guy sat in the middle of the fourth sofa, man-spreading and talking to a couple of other guys on his left. The woman on his right was sitting on her own in a lounge chair, leafing through one of the hardcover books. Celeste felt her heart start to pound. That had to be Martina—she was dressed the way Truman had described her, in a charcoal suit with heavy-rimmed glasses and wiry hair. It was actually a great look.

This place didn't have table service, she knew, so she wouldn't get a drink unless she ordered it at the bar, but right now the conditions were ideal to make her move.

Celeste went to the end of the sofa, adjacent to Martina, and spoke to the man-spreader. "Shove on over, son."

"Anything for a beautiful girl," he said, and unsubtly ogled her cleavage as he shifted down. "Can I get you a drink?"

"No thanks."

She turned to Martina, who was watching them idly over her glasses.

"Thanks for meeting me here," Celeste said, rolling her eyes toward the guy behind her.

Martina glanced at him, and at his companions, then set the book she was holding in her lap. "It's good to see you."

Effectively shut out, the guys started talking to each other again.

Celeste said quietly, "Thanks for that."

"I know how it goes."

"I like your pin," Celeste said, and tapped her own copy of it on her shirt collar.

"Were you here that night?" Martina said, her tone brightening.

"It was a great party. I love it when they open the back room."

"Totally. It's a great place to meet women. Is that why you went?"

"I'm not on the market at the moment," Celeste said, holding her gaze. "But it was fun to dance with all those women. And that doesn't mean you and I can't have a conversation."

Martina sighed. "I knew you were too hot to be single."

"Stop it," she said, and reached to tap Martina's knee. "You need to get the prescription for your glasses checked."

"You stop it, with the false modesty."

"It's not false. I really don't think I'm all that."

"Well, you should accept it, sister—you're

gorgeous." Martina reached for the tumbler on the low table in front of them and took a drink.

She should hang out with women more often, Celeste thought, watching her. It was way better for her ego than spending time with men.

"You're dressed like you've just come from work," Celeste said.

"My office is around the corner. This is a good place to unwind while the traffic dies down. I'm Martina, by the way."

"Penelope."

"So what do you do, Penelope?"

"I work in an art gallery," Celeste said. "But to tell you the whole story, I'm going to need a gin and tonic."

Martina smiled. "I'll save your seat."

"What are you drinking?"

"This was a scotch and soda, but I have to drive. You could get me a plain soda water."

Celeste went to the bar to buy the drinks, and sat down again, chatting with Martina for a while, answering her questions about the art world, which she seemed to be interested in.

When Truman walked in, he was wearing his gold disco shirt with the loopy brown circles, and those jeans that fit him so well. After a quick look around, he stepped over to where they were sitting. Celeste saw a flash of recognition in Martina's eyes.

"Watch out," Martina said quietly. "I know this weasel."

"Actually, so do I," Celeste said.

"Hey," Truman said, and flashed them a goofy smile.

"What's going on?" Martina demanded, her cheeks flushed. "Is this some kind of setup?"

"It's not like that," Celeste said.

"Is he your boyfriend?"

"Oh, my god," Celeste cried, throwing her head back. "What a nightmare that would be. We work together."

"You're a PI too?"

"I work in an art gallery, like I said."

"Liar," Martina snapped.

"Nothing I've said to you is a lie. I just didn't tell you why I wanted to talk to you."

"As I told Mr. Truman today, I can't answer any of your questions about my employer—especially under these circumstances."

"You don't have to answer anything," Truman said. "Just listen for a few minutes."

"To what?" She glared at him. "This is my place, and I'm not leaving. You two, on the other hand, should get the hell out of here."

As her voice rose, the guy at the other end of the sofa turned to see what was happening.

"Go get a drink," Celeste said to Truman, and gestured toward the bar.

As he walked away, Celeste turned back to Martina. "I'm sure you feel shanghaied right now."

"Of course I do," she said, lowering her voice. "How did you find me? Did you follow me from work?"

"Truman was at that event too." She tapped the pin on her collar. "He was pissed that night because they wouldn't give him one."

"It was an event for women. He's not a woman."

"Right. But he recognized it when he met you. He thought you might come here again."

Martina was still frowning at her, but she seemed to accept the explanation.

"So you're flirting with me under false pretenses."

"I told you up front that I wasn't on the market."

Martina huffed and folded her arms. "I'm thinking he's the one with the story."

"He'll do a better rendering. I wasn't there for all of it."

Truman returned with a margarita in hand and sat next to Celeste, squeezing in beside the straight guy, who shot him a look but shifted over. He slurped at his drink, then set it on the table and leaned forward, eyeing Martina.

"I suppose you feel like we've shanghaied you," Truman said.

Martina's brow furrowed. "Are you two working from a script?"

"We've covered that," Celeste said to him, waving a hand. "Moving on."

"My client works for a Skid Row nonprofit," Truman said. "He's been watching the progress of A Cut Above."

Martina held up a palm. "Let me stop you right there. I know plenty about the opposition to the project. I've heard it all, and I have no influence over the design process."

"It's not about the project," Truman said. "Two days ago, this guy told me that he had some dirt on Irwin Jeffries. Yesterday he disappeared."

Martina eyed him for a moment. "Is that the name you asked me about in the office?"

"Dyson Norris."

She closed her eyes for a second and took a breath. When she opened them again, she looked tired. "I don't remember that name from Jeffries's calendar. What kind of dirt?"

"Personal stuff that would damage his reputation," Celeste said.

"Was this guy trying to blackmail Jeffries?"

"I think so," Truman said. "I know that's stupid, but it's no excuse to make someone disappear."

"Do you think Jeffries is capable of that?" Celeste said.

Martina eyed her. "You said no questions."

"I've read enough about Irwin Jeffries to know that he's classist, and racist, and misogynist," Celeste said. "I'm sure you see that every single day."

She reached for her glass and spoke quietly. "Pretty much, yeah." After a sip, she met Celeste's gaze. "I handle the office end of things, not the politics. Jeffries does all that himself. But I know he's a corrupting force in this town."

"You never heard that he was meeting with Dyson," Truman said, "but that doesn't mean it didn't happen. What was he doing yesterday?"

"He wasn't around the office. The agenda said he had personal engagements all day, which means he's not available. I don't have access to his private calendar, but it syncs with the one I can see and blocks out time periods so that I don't double-book him. All I can see is that he has a personal event."

"I bet he met with Dyson," Truman said, "and something happened. Maybe there's evidence on his computer—a record of the meeting, at least. Is there any chance you could let me into the office for a few minutes when he's not around?"

"No way," she said firmly. "It's not worth my job, or risking a criminal charge, and Jeffries wouldn't hesitate to do that. Plus there are always other people around."

"We could go in at night," Truman said. "Let's

walk over there right now."

"I can't do that," Martina said, and shook her head, then stood up. "I have to pee."

"Do you want me to come with?" Celeste said.

"No," she said flatly, and walked off.

"Is she going to bail?" Truman said, watching her walk away.

"If she does, we can't do anything about it."

"She didn't even question that Jeffries might make someone disappear."

"I caught that too," Celeste said grimly.

"Did you know that your bra is showing through your shirt?" Truman said, sipping his margarita. "Black under white. Isn't that why you're supposed to wear the same color underwear?"

"Truman, you weirdo—it's completely intentional. I'm working a look."

"Really?" He adjusted her collar, smoothing one of the wings. "I don't think I could pull it off."

"I know you couldn't. You're flat-chested, and this outfit requires curves."

Martina came back, looking calmer now.

"Here's the thing," she said as she sat down, leaning toward them. "Off the record, you're right, Jeffries is a toxic trash fire. When I first started working there, I was standing in front of his desk one day, waiting for him to wind up a phone call. When he hung up, he started raging about the 'spic' he'd been talking to. I'm Hispanic, right, like half the people in this town, and I'm standing right there."

"Racism isn't known for being rational," Celeste said.

"Jeffries was even angrier about the homeless. Like they're personally trying to sabotage A Cut Above. 'Goddamn criddlers,' he calls them. When that place is built, I'll be astonished if there's a single square inch of affordable housing."

"How will he pull that off?" Truman said. "The plans are already finalized."

"But they're not set in stone." Martina waved an arm. "Smear some more cash around, and change the details at the last minute. Go look at those soulless phallic symbols around the stadium if you want a preview of A Cut Above. They're supposed to have commercial space at street level, right, but every one of them has forty vertical feet of parking lot at the sidewalk instead. Under the new codes, that's not supposed to happen anymore."

"Those really are nasty," Celeste said. "It completely isolates pedestrians from the building. Walking past, you feel like you're in a box canyon."

"Or a prison yard," Martina said. "Anyway, I'm not going to let you in to snoop around. If you were employed there, however"—she paused to eye them both—"you could do all the digging you want."

"How would I get a job in your office?" Truman said.

"Not you. Jeffries only hires women for clerical jobs."

Truman frowned. "Can he do that?"

Martina looked at Celeste and raised her eyebrows.

"I already have a job."

"I have some personal days banked," Martina said, "and I'm feeling a family emergency coming on. I could set you up with the temp agency that the company uses, and then ask for you to be my replacement for a few days."

"Wouldn't that be the same as just letting us in?" Truman said.

She shook her head. "The woman who runs the temp agency will be grateful for the referral, because the labor market is so tight right now, and she'll appreciate the directed request because it makes her job easier. Jeffries will never get wind of any of that, and my hands stay clean. If you get busted, it's on you."

Celeste bit her lip before she spoke. "I guess if it's only for a day or two. Saffron won't care."

"Great," Truman said, and to Martina, "The sooner the better—when can we set it up?"

"Tomorrow, if you want." She eyed Celeste. "The temp agency is run by a woman named Mrs. Lee. The 'Mrs.' part is important—she's attached to it. I'll tell her you've worked for Jeffries before, but not in the head office. You worked on a construction site by the stadium, like, a year ago. That way no one will wonder why they don't remember you."

"What kind of work did I do there?" Celeste said.

"Office stuff. Signing for deliveries, cutting checks sometimes, phoning and emailing vendors when they're late."

"It won't matter that I haven't worked in the main office?"

"Jeffries won't care, as long as there's someone with two X chromosomes to make him coffee. Steel yourself for dealing with him—you're going to be a girl again." She lowered her voice and mimicked him. "'Call my girl. She'll set it up.'"

"I can handle that," Celeste said. "Tell me about the office."

Martina described the kind of work Celeste would have to do, and how the company's data was stored. "I have no idea how to get into his private calendar, though, or even where you'd start a search for what you want."

"Who's the woman on the reception desk?" Truman said.

"Reggie. She's hard and petty, but not very bright. Be deferential to her and it'll go fine. I'll call Mrs. Lee at seven tomorrow and get things started. After that, I'll let you know." Martina pulled her phone out of her jacket pocket. "I'll need your number."

Celeste recited it as she thumb-typed.

"Is it really Penelope?"

Celeste met her gaze. "It is."

"Mrs. Lee will need your surname."

"De la Torre. Three words."

Martina nodded as she typed, then stood up and tucked the phone away.

"I really appreciate this," Truman said, rising with her.

Martina eyed Celeste. "If you're ever single again, you owe me one."

After she left, Truman said, "Another round, Pen-Pen?"

"Don't call me that. And I'd better not—it sounds like I might have to be up early."

Truman drained his margarita, then followed her out into the cool evening air. They walked toward where Celeste had parked.

"What did she mean, if you're single again?" Truman said.

"I told her nothing was going to happen, even though I was basically flirting with her."

"It worked. She flipped."

"That says something about her strength of character," Celeste said. "Choosing to help me even after I lied to her."

Truman affected Biff's tough tone. "Even a deadbeat heel can be cajoled into doing the right thing once in a while."

"She's not a heel. That's why I feel guilty about lying."

"I'm pretty sure she wants to jostle Jeffries as much as anyone. The guy sounds like a handful."

"So let's hope this plan works."

After she dropped Truman at his building, Celeste drove home and talked to Ernesto for a while before she climbed into bed. It took a while to fall asleep, thinking about infiltrating Jeffries's office, and all the subterfuge that would involve.

She heard Ernesto check the back door as he closed up the house for the night. It wasn't even clear what she was going to look for. But maybe it would be obvious once she got into Jeffries's office.

TEN

Celeste woke to María shaking her arm, a look of concern on her face.

"You're really out of it," she said, standing erect. "You slept through your alarm."

"Thanks," Celeste said, and stretched. That's what happens when you take a whole vike before bed.

María left, and Celeste checked her phone, but there was nothing yet from Martina. She could close her eyes again for a minute, she decided.

What seemed like moments later, her phone buzzed with a message. It came from a 323 number without a name attached, but it had to be Martina:

Expect a call soon from Mrs. Lee.

Before she had time to climb out of bed, the phone rang. Celeste sat up and cleared her throat before she answered.

After she'd introduced herself, Mrs. Lee said, "Martina tells me you've worked for Jeffries before."

"At a construction site near the stadium," Celeste said. "I can't remember the name of the project, but I ran the phones and cut checks to vendors."

"So you know the drill. You can operate a spreadsheet?"

"Of course."

"Can you come in to meet with me this morning?"

"Where's your office?" Celeste said, and typed the address into her phone once she'd ended the call. It wasn't hard to get to, over in Koreatown, although she'd have to pay for parking in that dense neighborhood.

Ernesto was long gone, she saw when she got up, even though it wasn't even 7:30. Most blue-collar work started at sunrise. María was in the kitchen eating toast and orange marmalade.

"Why are you up so early?"

"I'm doing some work with Truman. I won't be in the gallery for a day or two. Which reminds me—I should tell the owner."

María chuckled and rose to put some bread in

the toaster. On her phone, Celeste texted Saffron:

> Can't open the gallery today or tomorrow. Taking
> personal days.

María handed her a piece of toast on a plate, and she slathered it with the marmalade, chatting with her for a few minutes until María had to leave for work. After she'd rinsed her plate, back in her bedroom, Celeste saw that Saffron had responded to her text with an emoji that was stroking its chin—she was curious, but not concerned. Saffron could open the gallery herself if she needed to, but Celeste knew she didn't mind it sitting closed. It added mystique, she said, and the clients who bought from her were the kind of people who made appointments, not the ones who wandered in from the street.

From her closet she picked out conservative office drag that wasn't too dressy: a plain blouse and dark slacks. She added a pair of red-framed eyeglasses with plain glass in them, to make her look more like Martina, and bundled her hair back the way she had as well.

It would take longer to drive to K-town than to take the metro, the navigation app told her, so she walked the few blocks to the station and took the train. The tower at Mrs. Lee's address was close to the metro line under Wilshire Boulevard, and Celeste was soon stepping off the elevator and into her office.

"Penelope de la Torre," she told the woman on the front desk. "I'm here to see Mrs. Lee."

The woman herself soon appeared, wearing a dark-orange skirt and jacket, her black hair tied up with a sparkly pin. In her fifties, maybe, Mrs. Lee looked harried, and waved Celeste into her office.

Once Celeste was seated across the desk from her, Mrs. Lee asked her some cursory questions about her skills. More than probing her competency, it felt like they were designed to assess whether she was fully lucid and psychologically sound. When she asked for references, Celeste gave her the details for Truman and a couple of her cousins.

"Are you willing to be fingerprinted and submit to a background check?" Mrs. Lee asked.

"Of course."

She smiled. "Good—I'm not going to bother with that, but I wanted to see if you had anything to hide. I do need your tax information."

Celeste took the clipboard she handed across the desk and filled it out with her real details and name, adding "Penelope" in brackets. She might as well get paid for this.

When she handed it back, Mrs. Lee set it aside, not even glancing at it. "Are you available today?"

Celeste raised her eyebrows. "Actually, I am."

"That's a relief. Jeffries needs someone at the head office. Do you think you could go over now?"

"It's just a couple of metro stops. I can be there in a few minutes."

She recited the address and waited while Celeste typed it into her phone. "Did you ever meet the boss when you worked on the construction site?"

"I saw Irwin Jeffries there from time to time, but I didn't actually interact with him. Construction sites are intense."

Mrs. Lee nodded. "He needs a PA for a day or two. Just so you know, the guy is a total chauvinist. He probably won't chase you around the desk, but if he lays a finger on you, walk out and call me."

"If he tries to grope me, he'll have a black eye to worry about."

She waved a hand. "I get it, but don't tell anyone I condoned that."

———◆———

Waking later, Truman found a terse message from Celeste:

I'm in.

He smiled to himself. Hopefully there was something there to find. Once he'd made an espresso and felt like he could focus, he texted Ivy:

Can I see you this morning?

Her reply buzzed his phone soon after:

Come by my work.

The subsequent message had her office number and the floor it was on. Once he was dressed, Truman slung on his backpack and headed down the stairs, walking the bustling streets toward the central library. From the lobby he took the elevator up, and found the right room, and knocked on the door.

Ivy pulled it open and greeted him. She was dressed for work in another dark suit. Her desk shared a space with three others, and some bookshelves and map cabinets, but Ivy was the only one here now.

"Have you heard anything?" she asked him, and waved him to the chair beside her desk.

"I'm working on a couple of things. Where would Dyson go if he needed downtime?"

Ivy frowned. "That's not what's happening. He hasn't been home. I talked to his roommate again this morning."

"Tell me anyway."

She sighed impatiently. "Dyson doesn't like WeHo. There's a bar he goes to in Compton with lots of B-boys, and one near the central market on Hill Street."

"I know that place," Truman said. "That would be in the evening. What about during the day?"

"I don't know if he was serious about it, but he was reading a book about UFOs that talked about places around the city. He said he wanted to do a tour of them."

"Cover-up sites," Truman said. That's what the bookstore clerk had called them.

"You know about this?" she demanded.

"Just the broad strokes. I think they're places where UFO researchers died or disappeared."

"And now Dyson is missing."

"It can't be connected," Truman said. "No shadowy government agency would have nabbed him for reading about flying saucers. It has to be about Jeffries."

"You said you couldn't get to him."

"I have an operative who got a temp job in Jeffries's office. She should be there now. With any luck she'll get a chance to poke around."

"Seriously?" Ivy sat back in her chair. "Truman, that's amazing."

"I thought maybe Dyson's name would be on an appointments list," he said. "If we find something like that, you could take it to the police. But I don't know if we'll actually find anything."

"Still, you're the only person besides me who seems to give a damn."

"I wish I could get a look at that UFO book."

"Strangely enough," Ivy said, her brow furrowing, "you're in a library. I can look up the section where you'll find the people's copy."

"Dyson's copy had a bunch of notes in it. I doubt he left it at his office—it got stolen from there once."

"That's the book you found for him? Dyson hid the memory card in the UFO book?"

"Exactly."

"If he didn't take it with him, it might be at his apartment."

"Do you have a key?" Truman said.

"No, but his roommate will be there. He's always there. His name is Bug."

"I bet his mother didn't give him that name."

"It's a street name," she said, waving dismissively. "Because his eyes bug out when he's excited. I can introduce you by text if you want to go look for that book, but I have to send him a photo of you."

"Why?"

Ivy shrugged. "The guy is paranoid." She held up her cell phone and said, "Smile a little, so you look nonthreatening." Peering at the screen, she added, "Smile like it doesn't hurt."

Truman took a breath and tried to relax.

"I'll tell him you're a detective, and that you're looking into Dyson's disappearance. He'll love that." She spent a minute tapping on her phone before she looked up. "What are you going to do with the memory card if it's still in the book?"

"What do you think I should do with it?"

"You already know what the contents are."

Truman frowned. "I'm not going to try to extort Irwin Jeffries, if that's what you're thinking."

"If my worst fears are valid, that didn't work out very well for Dyson."

"I can't really erase it or even give it to you. If I find it, I'll hang onto it until we talk to Dyson."

"The honorable detective," Ivy said, holding his gaze.

"It's not about that. The card isn't mine to give away, and nothing about it is illegal, so I have no right to destroy it."

"Fine," she said flatly, and waved a hand.

"Dyson's apartment is in South Park, he told me. What's the address?"

Ivy rattled it off. "If you're comfortable with Skid Row people, you'll be just fine down there."

———•———

When Celeste climbed up out of the metro station in the Financial District, she stopped at a burrito place for a quick lunch, then fished a Ritalin tablet out of her bag and popped it under her tongue before she headed to Jeffries's office. It would help her steel herself for the task ahead.

Study buddies, they'd called them at college, and the drug definitely sharpened things up.

As she stepped off the elevator on forty-two, she eyed the JEFFRIES logo. It wasn't flashy, but the heavy letters and the modernist style were meant to imply gravity, and wealth, and power. Pushing inside, she caught sight of the receptionist, wearing a suit jacket, her hair in a ratty updo. Reggie. She looked tough, in a street kind of way. Martina had warned her to tread lightly with this one.

"My name is Penelope," Celeste said, and smiled sweetly. "Mrs. Lee sent me over to fill in for Mr. Jeffries's PA."

"We've been waiting for you," she said, giving Celeste the once-over. As she rose, Reggie gathered a sheaf of paper. "I'll show you to your desk."

Reggie led her into the corridor on the right, then into a tidy office with another door on the opposite wall. It was a small space, but it had a tall window with a great view toward the southwest.

"I wrote down the logins and passwords for the servers," Reggie said, and handed Celeste a sheet with a list of them. Holding her gaze, she added, "Don't leave that lying around."

"Of course," Celeste said, and glanced at the page. It was a printout from a spreadsheet. She set the paper on the desktop. If Reggie was really concerned about security, she wouldn't have typed them up in the first place. But these might turn out to be extremely useful.

"The copy room is on the other side of my office," Reggie continued. "There's a kitchen over there too. I'll introduce you to the boss. He takes his coffee with one cream, two sugars. Real cream only—none of that soy nut crap. It's in the fridge."

"Got it."

Reggie knocked on the other door and paused for a moment before she pushed it open. Jeffries's office was spacious, with a desk and a dark-wood credenza and lots of floor space. Windows lined two walls for sweeping views south to the stadium. Jeffries had put up some of those residential towers that loomed in the middle distance—it must be gratifying to look at them every day from his desk.

A man in a dark-green suit was standing at the window, a cell phone held to his ear. When he turned to face them, Celeste realized it was Irwin Jeffries. He was shorter than she'd imagined. His gray hair was slicked back, and his skin was rough and ruddy, unlike in the carefully filtered portrait provided to the media.

"Mr. Jeffries, this is Penelope," Reggie said. "She's filling in for Martina."

"That's fine," Jeffries said, and looked her up and down, not even trying to be subtle about it, as Reggie left through a different door.

"It's nice to meet you," Celeste said.

"Do people call you Penny?"

"If you'd like. I'm not fussy."

"Where are you from?"

"Boyle Heights," Celeste said, and gestured toward the east, even though that neighborhood wasn't in view of these expansive windows.

Jeffries waved impatiently. "I mean, where are you really from?"

She knew what he meant—Celeste didn't share his ethnicity, which meant she had to be an outsider, a foreigner. The appropriate response would be to repeat "Boyle Heights," and ask him where he was really from. But for things to go smoothly, she had to acquiesce to his biases.

"I know that my mother's people came from the ranchos of Zacatecas and Durango."

"That's *may-hee-coe*, right? I thought so."

Celeste flashed him a sweet smile.

"Listen," he said, taking a step closer. "I've got a meeting here in half an hour or so with some fucktards from a concrete company. You'll see it in the agenda. I need you to welcome them, be all friendly, and show them into the boardroom."

"Right," Celeste said, and nodded, making a mental note to find out where the boardroom was.

"Make them coffee if they want it, and all that jazz," he said, then jabbed a finger at her. "But no extras. They might try to sneak in some lawyers. I'm only going to talk to the three that are named in the appointment. One of them is a Chinaman."

"Got it," Celeste said firmly.

Jeffries cracked a smile. "You'll do just fine, honey."

"Do you need a coffee before the meeting?"

"Not now," he said, and waved her away.

There was nothing personal about the personal assistant position, she thought, stepping back into Martina's office. That label was a modern euphemism for what the job really was—an old-school secretary. She remembered María's documentary the other night. So this is what 1957 felt like.

———◆———

Before he left the library, Truman checked the map on his phone for Dyson's apartment. The easiest way to get there was to take the metro to USC and then walk. On the train he had to stand, but it was just a few stops, and he got off at the glittering gated private campus, with its lush lawns and ersatz classical statuary, and walked east, under the freeway, to be instantly confronted with the opposite end of the economy. Concrete and razor wire replaced grass and topiary, tents lined the sidewalks in front of the commercial buildings and fenced-in vacant lots, and the hardscrabble apartments had bars on all the windows. The contrast was dramatic, like Jeffries's luxury condos towering over Skid Row.

The neighborhood differed from his own in that it was mostly residential, and overall it felt like there were probably fewer tents and shopping carts. He found Dyson's address, one of those long and narrow four-upstairs, four-downstairs apartment buildings that had been built all over the city in the 1950s. This one needed some maintenance—a coat of paint, at least.

Truman trotted up the outdoor stairs and along the railing to the last apartment, farthest from the street, and knocked loudly.

The door opened a few inches, and an eye peered out at him above the chain. Presumably this was Bug.

"Can I help you?" he asked.

"I'm Truman."

"OK," he said dubiously.

"I'm a friend of Dyson's. Ivy told you about me this morning."

Finally he closed the door to disconnect the chain, then opened it wider. Bug was tall and thin, with short natural hair. He was darker than Dyson and Ivy, and was wearing a tank top and cargo shorts.

"I'm Bug," he said, suspiciously looking him over.

Truman stepped inside. This was the kitchen. It hadn't been renovated in a long time—the cabinets might even date to the 1960s, and the floor was a checkerboard of worn black and white linoleum tile.

"How do you know Dyson?" Bug asked.

"I met him at a festival in Gladys Park. On Skid Row."

His brow furrowed. "Did you sleep with him?"

"That's none of your business," Truman said firmly.

"How do you know Ivy?"

"Through Dyson. I met her at his office."

"Are you a federal agent?"

"Dude," Truman said. "Do I look like a federal anything?"

He folded his arms. "Yes or no."

"No," Truman said flatly.

Bug took a deep breath. "That's a relief. Federal agents can't lie about their job."

"That's so not true. They lie all the time. That's how they trick immigrants into opening the door so they can be deported. They tell them they're from the gas company and there's a gas leak, or that they're inspectors from the DWP."

Bug frowned. "Is that true?"

Truman gestured helplessly. "Yes."

"Damn it," he snapped.

"I'm sorry to burst your bubble."

Bug sighed. "You know, in the grand scheme, it's OK. Knowledge is power."

"So when did you last see Dyson?"

"When he left here Tuesday morning," Bug said. "I think he came back that afternoon, but I was out for a couple hours. There's been no sign of him since then."

"Did he tell you where he was going?"

"I thought he was just going to work, like always. He texted me that evening to say he was headed out of town for a few days, and not to worry."

"Can I see the message?"

Bug pulled out his phone and tapped at it, then held it for Truman to read. It was time-stamped around the same time he'd called Ivy and his office.

Once he'd read through it, Truman said, "Can I see his room?"

Stepping into the hall, Bug pushed open the first door. There was a neatly made bed against the wall under the window, and a desk with a laptop and a flatbed scanner. On the floor was a banker's box piled with shiny gray and orange-brown strips with perforated edges—the negatives Dyson had bought in Oregon.

"Did you look at his computer?" Truman asked.

"I tried—it's password protected. It's weird that he didn't take it with him."

"Not if he thought he was coming back soon."

"So you think someone got him."

"I don't know."

Paper and books were stacked on the desk, including *Saucers over the Southwest,* right on top. Truman picked it up, tempted to check for the memory card, but he wasn't going to do that with Bug watching him. Pulling open the cover, he found the former owner's *Birth of Venus* book-plate. This was the same copy. Flipping through it, the sticky notes were still intact.

"Do you think that'll be helpful?" Bug said.

"Dyson marked some addresses. It seems there's some remarkably deep research in this book."

"I know—I read it. He's not at any of those places. They got him."

Truman looked up. "Who did?"

"The government," Bug said intently.

He watched him for a moment. "Did he visit any of these places before?"

"Not yet. Dyson knew it was risky. If you're planning to go, turn off your phone."

"Why?"

"Do you know what a data harvest is?" Bug said.

"Explain it to me."

"Your cell carrier and all your apps keep track of where you are, and everything you look at, and everything you do. They sell it to data brokers, who mostly sell it to advertisers, but the police and the three-letter agencies use it extensively to track people."

"They track people who go to UFO sites? Lots of these addresses are in the middle of the city. Thousands of people go to them all day long."

"If you visit more than two of those sites, and the software notices that, they'll pick you up for questioning."

"They who?"

Bug threw up his hands. "Whatever agency enforces saucer secrecy. I don't even know if it has a name. One guy online says that he did the tour, and then for months black helicopters hovered over his house every single night."

"I wouldn't even notice," Truman said. "I live in the Fashion District. There are police helicopters overhead all the time."

"These are different. Quieter. They don't have any markings, and the windows are tinted black. Whatever you do, don't shine a laser pointer at them."

"That sounds like sage advice," Truman said, and gestured with the book. "I'm going to borrow this."

"Fine," Bug said, watching him stuff it into his backpack. "If you find Dyson, tell him to call me."

ELEVEN

It didn't take Celeste long to find the board-room, after asking Reggie, who frowned in annoyance at the interruption and pointed out the double doorway off the reception area. Celeste poked her head into the empty room and then took a minute to examine the art inside—three canvases on the wall opposite the window. It was stuff that might have been innovative in the early 1960s, but people purchased these now as a safe investment that could sit around and not lose value, like Treasury bonds or a brick of platinum. A bean counter had picked these, not an art person.

Celeste walked through reception again, and made sure to greet Reggie, even though what she threw back was indifference. It didn't matter, she reminded herself. As long as Celeste was affable, she wouldn't be considered a threat.

Just as she sat down at Martina's desk, the phone warbled, and Celeste picked up the receiver.

"Mr. Jeffries's twelve-thirty is here," Reggie said.

Celeste pulled up the calendar to get the approved names. One of them was Iwasaki—that must be the guy that Jeffries thought was Chinese. Striding into the reception area, she was relieved to see there were only three of them, all men, all in business suits.

"Gentlemen," she boomed, and flashed a broad smile, then shook hands with each of them, making sure the names matched what was in the calendar. Luckily these were the three who were expected for the meeting—Celeste didn't have to play the heavy and try to eighty-six a lawyer.

She led them into the boardroom and got them seated around the table.

"Who wants coffee?" she asked.

They all seemed surprised. Iwasaki said, "If you're making it for yourself, I'll have one. Just black."

Celeste smiled as she stepped out and walked to Jeffries's office. Iwasaki was a bona fide twenty-first-century man. She knocked on the door and stepped inside. Jeffries was at his desk, studying a sheaf of paper.

"Your concrete guys are in the boardroom," she said. "Just the three of them—no lawyers tagged along. I'll take them coffee."

"That's fine," he said, glancing up briefly.

"Do you need me in there with you to take notes or anything?"

"Nope," he said, not looking up again.

When she'd glanced into the little kitchen earlier, Celeste had noticed a bulbous carafe of coffee sitting on a burner. No way would she drink that stuff herself, as it had been sitting there fermenting all day, but at least it was already made for Iwasaki. Looking for a mug, she pulled open a cupboard door, and then another.

Behind her, from the doorway, a man's voice asked, "Looking for something?"

Celeste turned to meet his gaze. He was in his mid-thirties, maybe, and good-looking, with a square jaw and that mousy brown hair that so many Anglos had. At least he did his best with it, keeping it swept back and cut to look stylish. This was definitely a white-collar guy, not one of the construction-site managers, as he was wearing a collared shirt and suit pants.

She made her eyes wide. "Not at all. I was hired to inspect the cabinetry."

As she turned away to open another door, the guy chuckled. "I guess that was a stupid question."

Celeste ignored him, finally locating a mug and pulling it out to pour acrid steaming coffee into it.

"I haven't seen you here before," he said. "My name is Flint."

"You won't see me again either. I'm just a temp."

"I heard Martina was out. What's your name?"

"Penelope," she said, setting the carafe back on the burner. She gestured to the doorway with her free hand. "I've got work to do."

He grinned and stepped aside. "Can I come and talk to you later?"

"You seem to be able to walk, and your voice box works," she said, stepping past him, "so I'd say it's technically feasible."

"Aren't you a tough cookie."

Not responding to that, Celeste returned to the boardroom and set the mug in front of Iwasaki.

"Mr. Jeffries will be with you shortly," she told them.

Back at reception, Celeste stopped in front of the desk. "So how's your day going, Reggie?"

"Adequately," she said, briefly glancing up at her.

Celeste lowered her voice. "So who's the guy named Flint?"

"You don't need to bother with him. He's Mr.

Jeffries's son. Technically he's the vice president of operations."

"Good to know. I'll stay out of his way."

———◆———

On the train back downtown, Truman managed to get a seat. With his bag in his lap, he pulled out Dyson's heavy book. Folding it open, he held it up to the daylight from the window and peered into the gap along the spine. The memory card was gone. Pulling out his phone, he sent Ivy a text:

Found the book. The card isn't in it anymore.

He hadn't really looked closely at the contents of the weighty volume before, and flipping through it now, he found there were a lot of illustrations—sketches of saucers and alien bodies, photocopied maps annotated by hand, black-and-white landscape photos. It felt intense, as there were images of government documents stamped SECRET, many with blacked-out redactions, and grainy photocopied letters, even death certificates.

Dyson's sticky-note annotations marked several specific addresses, and the surrounding paragraphs explained why they were significant in the grand scheme, as Bug called it. They were all over the Southwest, some specified by latitude and longitude, some by street numbers. The local ones were scattered around the metropolis. Lots of them were too far afield to visit easily, but one was near the metro line in Hollywood—that would be his first stop.

Shifting down in his seat to get more comfortable, Truman dug into the story. A guy named Dewitt was writing a book that was going to reveal the Navy's involvement in retrieving a crashed saucer in the desert of northern New Mexico. Somehow Dewitt had obtained the relevant internal documents from the Navy. The book was set to be published in 1963.

Truman sighed. All this had happened long before Dyson or Truman had been born. It was hard to believe it was in any way meaningful now. Looking up, he saw that the train was pulling in at Seventh Street. He disembarked and followed the crowd down the stairs to the platform for Hollywood.

Once he was sitting on the next train, he read more about Dewitt. It seems the guy had been friendly with his landlady, Kathryn. One night in 1963 Kathryn heard a scuffle upstairs in his apartment along with cries for help. After she called the police, she ventured up to his rooms, and found that Dewitt had hung himself. The next day, three guys in dark suits showed up, claiming to be relatives, and said they wanted to pack up Dewitt's things. Kathryn let them in, and when she checked the apartment later, found that they hadn't taken anything except paperwork and notebooks.

Truman looked up at the gray concrete of the tunnel wall flashing past the window. Bug was totally paranoid, but maybe there was a reason. The copious trail of data everyone generated was useful in tracking people down, he knew, and all it took was one bureaucratic request to flag anyone who visited these places. With no human labor involved, the software would monitor the data stream—effortlessly, patiently, indefinitely. He pulled out his phone and put it in airplane mode.

When he flipped to the next page, he found a photo of Dewitt, who looked like an ordinary guy, in his shirtsleeves, his hair in an unctuous mid-century style. The author had also included a photo of the front of the apartment building, an old Victorian with a porch and narrow-board siding.

By the time he got to Hollywood, Truman understood the gist of Dewitt's story. He climbed up out of the ground and crossed Sunset Boulevard, then headed down a side street, toward Dewitt and Kathryn's address. As he got closer, he could see the two-story structure was gone, replaced with a much larger apartment building that spanned several of the original lots. It wasn't even new anymore. Based on the architectural style, it dated to maybe the 1980s.

Truman stood on the sidewalk and looked over the building. Dewitt and Kathryn were long forgotten here. If Dyson had ever visited this place, he wouldn't have lingered.

———◆———

After she left the boardroom, Celeste sat at Martina's desk and looked through Jeffries's office calendar on the computer. Some events had lots of detail, like the names for the meeting with the concrete guys, but chunks of some days were blocked out as "Personal." Martina had said those were placeholders from Jeffries's private calendar, which he kept elsewhere. Several long stretches of Tuesday were marked that way, as well as a two-hour block last night. Using her phone, she snapped a photo of the screen that showed this week's events.

Next she dug around on the company's servers. It was possible to access lots of stuff—contracts, and planning documents, and reams of building codes, along with back-and-forth correspondence with the building departments of a dozen local cities—but there was nothing personal, and nothing about Dyson.

Even the files about A Cut Above contained no record of the community pushback, only procedural stuff like documentation of the environmental review, the plumbing and electrical layout, and blueprints of the building. The side-view drawings showed three levels of parking up from the sidewalk before the housing started, even though creating soulless pedestrian-hostile zones like that was supposed to be illegal.

Buried deeper, Celeste found full-color renderings of the building. The view from street level had mature trees and happy people superimposed on the sidewalk in front of a monolithic bare concrete wall, with one dark opening in it for the cars to come and go. Scalies, designers called these little people, as they provided the human scale in the illustration. Despite their carefree smiles, overall this building felt really oppressive.

Flint stepped in from the hallway and flashed her a smile.

"Hey, Penelope," he said. "I feel like we got off on the wrong foot."

"You called me a cookie. If your name wasn't on the front door, I would have slapped you."

"Because it's sexist?"

"Would you call a man a cookie?" she demanded.

Flint considered that. "Probably not."

"So there's your answer."

"I apologize for my ignorance," he said. "Maybe you've taught me something today."

Celeste eyed him closely, trying to decide if there was any shred of sincerity there, or if he was just messing with her.

"You're welcome." She gestured to the door. "I've got work to do."

———•———

Truman found a coffee place on Sunset and sat in the window with a steaming cup of espresso. The flying-saucer book cited another address near here, and the accompanying text described an event that had gone down in 1976. That was more recent than the last one but still ancient history in a town with so much perfunctory architectural churn. Propping the book against the glass, he read the details.

It was the same kind of story, about a UFO researcher named Foster. His neighbor, a man named Collier, who owned the duplex they lived in, heard a commotion and found Foster unconscious on the floor, bleeding from the head. The room was torn up like there had been a brawl. Foster died a few days later in the hospital, but strangely, his death certificate, reproduced on a full page of the book, listed his cause of death as cancer.

After Foster's funeral, a guy in a dark suit showed up at his place. Collier noticed him on the doorstep and confronted him. The guy said he was collecting personal items and valuables, and showed him that he had a key. When Collier went in later, the place had been ransacked. He didn't know if anything had been taken, but Foster's wallet was sitting out on the table, with cards and cash intact.

It got weirder—Foster's phone number had been published in a 1970s UFO newsletter. Six years after he died, when *Saucers over the Southwest* was being written, the number was still registered to the dead man. When the author called it at various times over the course of a couple of years, the response was either silence, with a series of clicks on the line, or a recording of a woman's voice reciting a string of numbers.

The author's theory was that the Navy had kept the line connected as a trap for Foster's associates—they could trace who was calling, then stalk that person at their leisure. Truman gazed out at the traffic rolling by on Sunset and considered that. It seemed like an awful lot of effort.

The phone number appeared in one of the illustrations in the book, a reproduction of the ad that Foster had taken out asking for UFO tips from government insiders. It was in the 213 area code, like the whole city was back then, and the first two digits were familiar too, from an even earlier era when telephone exchanges had names—46 corresponded to HO for Hollywood.

The strangeness had happened decades ago, but no way was Truman going to dial that number, as tempting as it was. Pulling out his phone, he reconnected to the cell network, then pulled up a map to check the address where Foster and Collier had lived. The duplex was still there, based on the street view. Once he'd put the device in airplane mode again, he drained his espresso and packed up the book.

It was less than a metro stop away—he'd get there just as quickly walking, he decided, and headed east. This part of Hollywood had been slower to gentrify, and the residential street was still mostly duplexes and small apartment buildings. The only new structure on the block, a three-story full-lot mansion, was still under construction. Despite the high chain-link fence surrounding the site, the concrete walls of the first floor had been heavily graffitied, a clear expression of the neighborhood's feelings on being displaced by wealthy newcomers.

The duplex looked much like it did in the black-and-white photo in the saucer book. The cladding was different, and the yard had a fence around it now, but the roof lines and the porch columns were the same.

The fence had a gap in it where a narrow concrete walk led to the dual front doors. Truman stepped into the yard and stood on the walk, gazing at the building. The book hadn't explained which unit Foster had lived in and which was Collier's.

A moment later a woman with dark hair and a red print dress stepped out one of the front doors and called to him in Spanish.

"Sorry, *no entiendo*," Truman said.

"Can I help you?"

"I was just looking at the house."

"Why?" she demanded.

"A man named Collier owned it in the 1970s."

"Well, I own it now."

"Can I show you a picture?"

She folded her arms as Truman dug out his phone to find the photo of Dyson, glad that it came up without the need to reconnect to the network. He walked toward the front step and held out his phone so the woman could see the screen.

"Have you ever seen him around?"

"He's good looking," she said, raising her eyebrows. "I'd remember him."

"Did you ever hear about Collier, or a guy who lived here named Foster?"

"I've been here fifteen years, and I never heard of any of them."

"Do you still have a landline?"

"Is this guy missing or something?"

"I thought he might have come around here."

"I can't help you," she said, and went inside, pulling the heavy metal screen door closed.

———◆———

When Irwin Jeffries stepped into her office, Celeste looked up and smiled.

"How was your meeting?"

He waved dismissively. "I've got those cocksuckers on the ropes."

"Good to hear."

"Listen—I'm going to a job site."

"Am I coming with?"

"That's not necessary. I'm just giving you a heads up. See you tomorrow."

"Have a good evening," Celeste called after him as he left.

She waited a few minutes before she got up and went into Jeffries's oversize office. The room was empty, and she had to work to pull her eyes away from the dramatic sweeping view of the city. Sitting at his desk, she woke his computer, but as expected it was locked with a password. Celeste looked under the blotter, and in the desk drawers, even under the lamp—all the places where people wrote down hard-to-remember login details. But Jeffries wasn't that lax—his password wasn't recorded anywhere.

She walked over to the file cabinets that lined the wall and pulled one open. The folders seemed to be arranged alphabetically, and most sounded like the names of companies, although there were also some personal names. One of the tabs that caught her eye was labeled IWASAKI. Pulling it out, she found that it contained just a few pages that looked to have been printed from a website. Scanning the contents, it was a biography of the guy from the concrete company, with his schooling and work history and professional affiliations—basic intel. She stuffed the file back in its place.

What was Dyson's last name? Celeste closed her eyes for a moment to try to remember. Truman had said it to Martina. She visualized sitting on the sofa in that little bar, and soon it came to her—*Norris*.

Two drawers down she found the N's, and she took a deep breath when she saw a tab labeled NORRIS, DYSON. The folder was thin, she saw, as she pulled it out. Kneeling on the floor, she set it on the carpet and flipped it open. There were just two pages. On top was a receipt from a cellphone store, for a new phone, dated two days ago—the day Dyson had disappeared. Pulling out her own phone, Celeste held it over the sheet and photographed it.

The only other page in the folder was a printout of an email from a bank. The subject line read "Confirmation of change to credit card account," and the body text said simply "Authorized users: Dyson Norris."

Martina had said she didn't recognize Dyson's name, so she wasn't the one who'd compiled this file. The name on the tab had been written by hand, in block letters that ran together, as if the scribe had been in a rush. Jeffries was tightly wound and impatient—maybe he'd done it himself.

After she photographed the second sheet, she slipped the file back into the drawer and tucked her phone away. At that moment the office door flew open, making her start. She looked up to see the green suit. When he caught sight of her kneeling beside the open drawer, Jeffries stopped in his tracks.

"What are you doing?" he demanded.

"Mr. Jeffries—I thought you were gone."

"Well, I'm back."

"I was going to type up your notes from that meeting with the concrete people," Celeste said. "Did you file them under one of their surnames, or under the name of the company?"

Jeffries watched her for a moment, his eyes sharp, then waved a hand. "Don't worry about that. It's not necessary. I don't even take notes."

Celeste rolled the drawer closed and stood up. Stepping past her, Jeffries went to his desk, leaning over it to wiggle the mouse and peer at the screen. As she walked out, Celeste could feel the blood pounding in her ears, the heat in her face. That had been close.

After he stepped back onto the sidewalk, Truman took a last look at the duplex. Across the street, in the yard fronting a bungalow, a guy stood staring at him, leaning on a rake. Truman ignored him, but before he had taken more than a few steps, the guy called, "Excuse me."

When Truman glanced at him, the guy furtively waved him over. He had a gardening implement in hand, Truman reasoned, and he didn't look homeless, wearing a green work shirt, and jeans, and a straw hat with a concave brim that obscured his face, so maybe he wasn't going to ask for spare change. Truman crossed the street, but as he got closer, and the guy shifted his hat up, he realized something was off. He was dressed like a gardener, but he couldn't be—this guy was Anglo.

"What's up?" Truman said, approaching the low iron fence.

"You were asking about Foster," the guy said quietly.

"You could hear that from over here?"

"I knew it," he said intently. "What do you know about Foster?"

"Only what I've read. He died long before my time." Truman eyed him for a moment. "What do you know about Foster?"

"Are you a federal agent?"

Truman sighed. "No."

"Good." He looked relieved. "Federal agents can't lie about their identity."

"So I've heard. Are *you* a government agent?"

"Of course not," he snapped.

"It must be true, then. So you're just standing here with a rake watching Foster's house?"

"I live here." The guy gestured behind him. "I didn't know about the history of the place across the street when I moved in, but I met some of the other people."

"What other people?"

"People who came to look—like you. People seeking the truth. UFO questers."

Truman pulled out his phone and found the photo of Dyson. "Did you ever see this guy?" he said, holding it out to him.

He leaned closer. "I can't say that I remember seeing him. I know I never spoke to him. Who is he?"

"A quester." Truman tucked his phone away. "I think they got him."

The guy's eyebrows shot up. "You mean …"

"Yup. He's been missing since Tuesday."

"Don't tell me about that," he said quickly.

"They're probably watching us right now." His eyes darted furtively around the street. "Go on, now. Get out of here." With that, he picked up the rake and turned to walk toward the house.

———◆———

Celeste didn't dare go back into Jeffries's office, as she wasn't sure if he'd left again—he would have gone out the other door. There was no reason for her to be here anyway if Jeffries wasn't, so maybe she should just leave. She briefly considered asking Reggie whether that was an option, but she was unlikely to get a straight answer from her. It was getting close to six—she'd leave then.

Flint stepped in from the hall, flashing that pretty smile. He was wearing a suit jacket now, with the same blue-gray luster as his pants.

"It's almost quitting time," he said.

"Aren't you in management?" Celeste said, leaning back in her chair. "That attitude isn't going to make you rich."

Flint waved a hand. "My father's already rich. I don't need to worry about that."

"It was nice of him to give you a job anyway. That way you don't have to play polo and drive around in sports cars."

He grinned. "Is that what you think of me?"

"I guess it's a type," Celeste said, and shrugged.

"You don't know me," he said firmly. "I came

in here to ask you out."

"How do you know I'm not married?"

"There's no ring on that finger. It was the fourth thing I looked at when I saw you in the kitchen today."

Celeste laughed. "Good answer."

"Finally," he said, throwing up his hands. "The ice cracks. So can we go get a drink?"

"We can," Celeste said, and sat up to lock the computer before she rose.

She closed the office door and walked out with him, through the reception area. Reggie glanced up, then did a double-take at the sight of the two of them together.

"Good night, Reggie," Celeste called to her.

No response came, but Celeste could feel her eyes burning holes in her back.

TWELVE

That paranoid neighbor didn't know anything more about Foster than what was in the book, Truman decided, walking to the metro station. He didn't recognize Dyson, but that didn't mean Dyson hadn't been there. Once he was on the train, he looked through the addresses Dyson had marked. The only other place Truman could get to without a car in a reasonable amount of time was downtown.

Truman read the story. At the dawn of ufology, meaning in the 1950s, there were regular meetups and lectures for people interested in the strange new phenomenon of flying saucers. From the beginning, dark forces were messing with researchers and the organizers of these events, most likely in an attempt to tamp down public interest.

The author quoted a book from the era that profiled several researchers who had been scared out of the field by shadowy figures uttering threats. The title was *They Knew Too Much about Flying Saucers*. Truman paused and looked absently at the throng of bodies on the platform outside as the train rolled to a stop. Where had he heard that before?

The bookstore clerk had said it, he remembered. She'd mentioned "people who knew too much about flying saucers." Maybe she'd used that phrase to test whether he really had any knowledge about the field, like a hidden password. He hadn't caught it. Truman grinned at the memory. It didn't really matter, but he'd failed her cryptic test.

Back in the book, he read that sometimes there was clear evidence that the interference was governmental, as the harassers were identifiable as military, usually the Navy. It was easy to scare people back then too—all they had to do was throw out accusations that a person was involved in communism. Anyone tarred with that brush could be blacklisted and shut out of academia, and government work, and corporate careers. But sometimes the harassers were eerily stilted and inhuman, and the assumption then, of course, was that they were aliens.

In 1957 a lecture had been planned for

ballroom C at the Baltimore Hotel, a grand old dame that still stood downtown. It had a great bar, and coffered ceilings, and so much mahogany wall paneling that they must have clear-cut half of Belize.

A day before the lecture, the author said, phone calls were made to strategic people—local UFO group leaders and journalists—telling them that the event had been canceled. Hours later, amid the growing confusion, more disinformation came, explaining that the cancellation was an error, and the event was on again, but an hour later and at a different venue, the philharmonic auditorium.

That was still a tactic bureaucrats used to stifle participation, Truman knew—he'd just read about it happening with a public meeting on Jeffries's condo project. Odd too that he'd been talking about that long-gone auditorium with Ivy just yesterday. They'd been sitting in a coffeehouse on that very site. Was that meaningful? He watched the concrete racing past the train window. He could imagine Bug, wide-eyed, explaining it to him: "It's all connected." But of course it wasn't. It couldn't be. This book was starting to seep into his psyche, and taint his rational mind. If he wasn't careful, he'd wind up like Bug, or the guy with the gardener's hat.

In 1957 the philharmonic auditorium wasn't

far from the Baltimore, but so much confusion had been generated that very few people turned up for the lecture at the correct venue. Standing at the back of the ballroom were several stern-looking tight-lipped guys in suits, presumed to be G-men, asking for names and taking notes on everything that was said.

The speaker for the event was so freaked out that he didn't say much, visibly nervous and sweating "like a horse," one attendee said. He refused to show the photographic evidence he had of saucers over the Mojave, and he left the venue early, slipping out the back way.

Turning the page, Truman found a photo of him from that day, his dark hair nattily coiffed, wearing a light seersucker suit, standing at an old-fashioned mike, a grim expression on his face. Other men stood behind him, some talking, some listening. The whole scene looked chaotic.

Truman folded the book closed and stuffed it into his backpack. The train was pulling into the station at Pershing Square, just a block from the hotel.

Striding into the lobby, he couldn't help but gaze upward to admire the century-old stained-glass ceiling. He stepped up to the reception desk.

"Can I look at one of the ballrooms?" he asked the clerk.

"You'll have to talk to the events coordinator,"

he said, meeting Truman's eye. "Her name is Ynez. The office is on the mezzanine."

"Where's the mezzanine?"

"One level up." He grinned and pointed across the room. "You can take that staircase."

At the top of the stairs, the hallway was much less grand than the public spaces below, but it retained the same antique vibe in the light fixtures, and the door frames, and the moldings. Truman found the right office—a dark wooden door with a frosted glass pane. Painted on it in gold lettering was EVENTS. He rapped on the wood, and heard a faint "Come in."

It was a crowded little room, he saw, stepping inside. Behind the desk, Ynez looked to be in her forties and was wearing a dark-red blazer with a gold nametag, like the staff at reception. Her black hair was tucked behind her ears.

She smiled and asked, "Can I help you?"

"I'm getting hitched this fall," Truman said. "We're in the initial planning stage, and I wondered if I could look at one of the ballrooms."

"Of course. We offer a full range of wedding services besides the venue itself."

"Maybe we can start with the room. I'll know right away if it's going to work."

"Is your bride available today?"

"Groom," Truman said. "He's working. He kind of assigned a lot of the planning to me."

Ynez nodded. "Excellent. Boy-boy weddings are the best."

"Why is that?"

"Because typically both parties want to go all out. With straight couples, it's usually just the bride."

Truman chuckled. "I can see that."

Ynez pulled open a desk drawer and grabbed a bundle of keys.

"Can I ask your name?" she said as she stood up.

"Ernest," he said. "Ernest de la Torre."

"*¿Habla español?*"

"Sorry, I don't."

"I didn't think so," Ynez said. "You don't look Latino."

"I guess my family assimilated long ago."

She led him to the stairs and down to the main floor, then into a long broad hallway.

"An old magazine I saw said that ballroom C was the one to look at," Truman said.

"We don't label them that way. They have the names of colors. The Taupe Room and the Chartreuse Room are popular for weddings. I can show you both."

"Do you know which one was ballroom C back in the day?"

"I can't say that I do." Ynez frowned in thought. "I know there have always been five of them, and they're all in a row. If they were named alphabetically, then logically ballroom C would be the one in the middle."

"Great—let's look at that one."

"The Chartreuse Room," she said confidently, and gestured farther down the hallway.

There was a liqueur with that name, Truman remembered, and he'd probably sampled it at some point, but he couldn't recall what it looked like.

"What color is chartreuse, exactly?" he said.

"You know the safety vests that the Caltrans workers wear when they're on the side of the freeway?"

"Actually, no. I don't drive a lot."

"OK—think of a tennis ball." She stopped to unlock a set of double doors.

"Kind of yellowy-green?" Truman said.

"Exactly."

She pushed open the doors, revealing a huge room. Truman wandered inside and took it in. There was a stage at the back, and chairs stacked at one wall. The carpet was modern, but there was lots of the original dark mahogany paneling, and a pair of glam chandeliers, and a florid ceiling mural. He tried to imagine it in 1957—the UFO guy up on the stage, nervous and sweating in his seersucker suit, with that old-fashioned mike, and the dark-suited spooks hanging around the back.

"Nothing in here is painted chartreuse," Truman said.

"It's just a name." Ynez stood by the door, letting him absorb the atmosphere.

"It's really beautiful."

"Seating capacity is four hundred. Would that accommodate all your guests?"

"I think so," Truman said absently, gazing at the ceiling.

"So what's your betrothed's name, Ernest?"

He looked at her. "My betrothed? Oh—uh, Dyson."

"Tell Dyson he should see this place too before you make any decisions."

"I have a picture of him," Truman said, and pulled out his phone, pulling up the head shot.

"Very handsome," Ynez said politely, glancing at the screen.

"Have you seen him around here? It was his idea to consider the Baltimore."

"He hasn't been to my office," she said, looking at the photo again. Her eyes narrowed. "Didn't he tell you whether he'd been here already?"

"He had so many ideas for venues." Truman shrugged. "It's hard to keep everything straight."

"Well, I can tell that you're impressed with the Chartreuse Room." She looked around the space. "You should bring him to see this."

"I'll do that. Thanks for showing it to me." He

turned and walked out into the hall.

"Would you like to see the Taupe Room?" Ynez said, locking the doors. "It's slightly smaller."

"I think I get the idea."

"If you'd like to come upstairs, I can run through some of the pricing. Have you set your dates?"

"We're really just in the initial phase right now."

"Take my card, at least," Ynez said, and pulled one from her jacket pocket. She met his gaze. "In case you hadn't figured it out already, I love weddings."

Truman glanced at it briefly as he thanked her, then tucked it in his bag. Once he was outside on the street, he pulled out his phone and switched off airplane mode. It felt foolish now, that he'd fallen for that little bit of paranoia. As if minor incidents from half a century ago, tragic though they were, still echoed in the present. More important, nobody had recognized Dyson—overall, this had been a totally fruitless afternoon.

THIRTEEN

Stepping off the elevator into the lobby of the office building, Flint asked Celeste, "Do you know the Baltimore?"

"I love the bar there," she said.

"It's close—we can walk."

As they went out to the street, she heard her phone buzz in her bag, and pulled it out to check. It was a message from Truman:

How was today? Debrief over tacos?

Celeste texted back:

As you often say, I'm working.

His reply made her smile:

So … many … men.

"Do you live around here?" Flint said, matching her pace as they walked abreast.

"In Boyle Heights."

"That's around here. You must have a quick commute."

"Where does the Jeffries dynasty reside?" Celeste said.

"I don't live with my father. He has an obscene palace in the hills. I have a condo on Ninth."

"In one of the glassy new buildings that your family business put up?"

"Oddly enough, yes."

"Sweet deal."

"So if you don't like rich people," Flint said, his tone affable, "why did you come out with me?"

"I don't have a problem with money itself, or even people who've amassed it. But I do find entitlement pretty grating."

"Do I act entitled?"

"I haven't decided yet," Celeste said.

Flint laughed at that, and held the door for her as they stepped into the Baltimore.

"Table or barstool?" Flint said, pausing on the threshold of the ornate room.

"The bar is more fun," she said, and they went over to the tall chairs.

As he sat down, Flint carefully flipped the tails of his jacket over the low back of the chair. A bartender in a black vest and bow tie stepped up. Squat and with broad shoulders, his hair was buzzed flat on top.

"Madam?"

"Gin and tonic," Celeste said.

"Oh—that sounds good," Flint said, leaning toward the guy and holding his gaze. "What kind of gin do you use?"

He laid out the options, and Flint nodded thoughtfully.

"I'm just worried that the top-shelf stuff will burn a hole in my wallet."

The guy leaned across the bar and spoke quietly. "Don't tell my boss I spilled the beans, but several of the cheaper brands taste exactly the same."

"You're a good man, César," Flint said. "I appreciate your candor. I think I'll just have a pint from the tap. Something dark."

Celeste had to grin, watching them interact. Flint had read the bartender's name on his little gold nametag, and had made a reasonable attempt to pronounce it the Spanish way, *say-zar.*

Once César had stepped away, Celeste said, "You don't seem like your father."

"I grew up with my mother," he said, swiveling toward her and gesturing with a hand. "They split when I was very young. Irwin only took an interest in me when I was old enough to hold an intelligent conversation. By then, it was too late for him to mold me in his own image."

"What's his image?"

"You've met him. He's a dick."

Celeste chuckled and looked to César as he set down their drinks. Flint handed him a credit card.

"Sometimes people have biases because they don't have enough information," she said.

"You don't have to minimize it for me," Flint said, and clinked his glass against hers. "I know he's a dick. He's been exposed to all the information the rest of us have, and he chooses to be a bigot anyway."

"So what's your image?"

"I went to school, but I never really felt a calling. I did business administration because that's what Irwin was willing to pay for. Before that I wandered around India for a while."

"That must have been eye-opening," Celeste said, and sipped her drink.

"I loved it there. It's like all the grunge is out on the streets, but people are more spiritually developed. Here the lawns get mowed, and the streets get swept, but inside, people are empty."

It was a canny insight, she thought, eyeing him. "You should swing by Skid Row. The streets don't actually get swept."

Flint chuckled and drank from his beer glass. "What about Penelope? What's your passion?"

"I'd have to say visual art. I studied art history."

"You should be working in that field."

"It's not especially lucrative."

"But you keep up on trends in the art world?"

"Absolutely."

"I should get your advice on investing in some art."

"With buyers, the first thing I do is ask a question," Celeste said. "Do you want art that's important, and groundbreaking, and timely, or do you want art that will appreciate in value over the next decade?"

Flint frowned. "It's not the same thing?"

"There's some overlap, but mostly it's a different set of artists."

He twisted his glass absently on the bar top. "I'm not sure how I'd answer."

"Your company's boardroom is a good example. Whoever acquired the paintings in there was an investor, not an aficionado."

"That's no surprise. Irwin would always go with the money."

They talked more about art, and about India. Flint was a surprisingly good listener. Eventually Celeste unpinned her hair and flipped it behind her ears. Flint watched her, a smirk on his lips.

"You have great hair," he said.

"It's a lot of work. Plus the expense. Sometimes I think I should just butch it."

"Please don't. Beautiful things take effort."

Celeste eyed him as she finished her drink. Almost as soon as she set down the glass, César appeared.

"Another round?"

"Not for me," she said.

"We could go eat," Flint said, and to César, "Just the check."

"Thanks," she said, "but I can't."

"Are you parked at the office? I can walk you back there."

"I'm on the metro," Celeste said, sliding off her chair.

Once Flint got his card back, they walked to the lobby and then out to the street.

"I'm headed that way," he said, pausing on the sidewalk and jabbing his thumb.

His gaze was intent, and focused on Celeste. That look in his eye—he was smitten, she realized. That didn't happen every day.

Celeste pushed her hair back. "I had fun."

"I'm glad," he said gently.

"So, were you going to kiss me good night?"

Flint smiled and leaned in, and she met his warm mouth. It tasted yeasty from the beer. As she got into it, she felt his hand on her shoulder. The guy was good at this. People walking by mostly ignored them, except someone who muttered "Hoo-wee." Leaning closer, Flint pressed his body against hers, and she reached inside his jacket, resting her hands on his waist. Finally Celeste pulled back.

"I really have to go," she said.

"I wish you'd come home with me."

"Another time. I'll see you at the office."

Flint sighed. "Good night, beautiful."

Walking the other direction, Celeste couldn't help but smile. It felt good to be the object of someone's desire. When she stopped at the corner, waiting for the crossing light with a cluster of other pedestrians, she pulled out her phone and texted Truman:

Ready to debrief.

As she reached the opposite curb, her phone buzzed with Truman's reply:

I just ate at the central market. Meet me at that place with the taxidermy?

That wasn't far. She texted him a thumbs-up and headed that way. A few minutes later she walked up the plaid-carpeted stairs into the barroom, dimly lit and lined with dark wood. Truman wasn't here yet, and it wasn't that busy, so she took a stool at the bar. The macabre antlered heads of several deer and a moose were mounted high on the walls, but sitting at the bar, she didn't have to look at them.

"A soda water, and a blended margarita," she told the bartender when she stepped over.

"Was it worth it?" the woman said, and furrowed her brow. Her fuchsia-tinted hair was cut in a bob, and her accent sounded vaguely Eastern European.

Celeste frowned. "What are you talking about?"

"Someone has disturbed madam's lipstick."

"Oh, god," Celeste said, sitting up. "Is there a mirror in the restroom?"

She nodded and shot her a wry smile. "I'll save your spot."

In the restroom she saw what the woman had been talking about—Celeste had worn a somber shade for a day of office work, but now it was smeared all over half her face. She spent a minute with a paper towel and the tube of lipstick repairing the damage, then went back to the bar. The bartender set the drinks in front of her.

"Totally worth it," Celeste said, and dropped a C-note on the bar.

In her bag she'd noticed a loose trank, and dug it out now, biting the tablet in half and dropping the other part back in. At that moment, Truman appeared beside her, and took the adjacent barstool.

"What was that?" he demanded.

"Greetings to you too," she said, and frowned.

"Don't bullshit me. You said you were going to get a handle on that."

"It's fine," she snapped. "I am handling it. I just need to wind down right now."

"Handling it yourself means you're never going to stop. Don't you think you might benefit from going to a meeting?"

She shook her head, pausing as the bartender stepped over to set down her change. "It's not like that, Tru."

"That's what every junkie says."

"I am not a junkie," she hissed. "Half an Ativan and some soda water is a lot less drugs than the tequila in your margarita."

"Fine," he said, and looked away. "I just wish you'd talk to someone about it."

Celeste waved a hand and sipped at her drink.

Truman picked up his margarita and clinked it against her glass before he took a sip. "You look like an office drone."

"I'm glad. That was the goal."

"You also look a little flushed. Who was the guy?"

"You can tell?"

"Just a guess," Truman said, "based on your text."

"I only kissed him. His name is Flint. We went for a drink after work."

"Score. He works for Jeffries?"

"He kind of is a Jeffries. He's Irwin's son."

"Seriously?" Truman said. "Are we sure that's not too close to the investigation?"

"You don't get to say that. You're the king of sleeping with your clients."

"No judgment," he said, and flashed his palms. "I just hope you can stay objective."

"How many times have I said that to you?" she demanded.

"A few." He looked away and slurped his margarita.

Celeste sighed. "Anyway, I couldn't get into all the digital files, but I found some significant evidence on paper. Irwin doesn't lock his file cabinets."

"What did you find?" Truman said, sitting up.

"A couple of things. Let me share these with you." She pulled out her phone and tapped at it.

Looking at his own screen, Truman studied the photo she'd taken of Jeffries's office calendar, and zoomed in on it. "Lots of unexplained personal time on Tuesday. That's when Dyson disappeared. There's also a personal event last night. There weren't any details?"

"He manages his private calendar himself," she said, "so I couldn't find out what he was doing, or where. The office calendar only shows that he was doing something."

"It might be useful anyway."

"Look at the other documents," she said, and

sipped her drink, then explained about finding the file folder with Dyson's name on it.

Truman broke into a broad smile as he zoomed in on them. "This is excellent news."

"It shows that Dyson took a credit card and maybe a phone from Jeffries. Doesn't that imply that Dyson is working for him?"

"It does, but both of these are dated Tuesday. That's the last time anyone saw Dyson. It means he's alive somewhere—Jeffries didn't ice him."

"It also means he's not the guy you thought he was," Celeste said. "He's working for the person he says he's working against."

"We don't know that yet. Maybe he's doing something constructive."

Celeste watched him for a moment. "Does Biff Sturgis talk about Occam's razor?"

"Not that I remember." Truman frowned. "What's that?"

"It's part of the scientific method. It means that the explanation with the fewest new assumptions is the most likely one. Ergo, Dyson is working for Jeffries."

"For now, let's give Dyson the benefit of the doubt. He's alive, so we can ask him to explain himself."

"If we can find him," Celeste said.

"You're in Jeffries's office. Maybe you could just ask him."

"If he suspected that's why I was there, he'd have me arrested, or at the very least, unceremoniously thrown out on my butt."

Truman pursed his lips. "That does sound like him."

"Did you notice that the receipt for the cell phone has the phone number on it?"

"You think we should call it?"

"Maybe it's a better option," Celeste said, and sipped at her soda water.

"There has to be a reason why Dyson dropped out of sight, and cut off communication. He won't want to talk to me."

"My cousin Blanca works for that provider. She might be able to track the phone's location."

"Can she just do that? What kind of job does she have?"

"She's a retail clerk." Celeste shrugged. "But it can't hurt to ask."

"We should do it in person. It'll be easier to persuade her."

"Her store is downtown on Seventh, right by the metro. Let me find out if she's there in the morning." Gazing at her screen, Celeste sent Blanca a text:

At work tomorrow?

Her response came a moment later:

From nine. Why?

"Good news—she'll be there," Celeste said to Truman, and texted a reply:

I'm going to drop in.

She added a kiss-blowing emoji, then asked Truman, "Can you be up early? We have a meeting with Blanca at nine."

"Great work." Truman tapped his glass against hers and took a drink. "I wonder if I should text Dyson's sister."

"We don't really know anything yet, except that he's probably still alive."

"You're right. Biff says, 'Play your cards close to the vest.' I actually saw her this morning," he said, and told her about meeting Ivy, and Bug, and getting sucked into his UFO paranoia, and then skulking around Hollywood.

"You must have been at the Baltimore right before I was. That's where I went with Flint."

"Even his name sounds butch. What does he look like?"

"Basic Anglo frat boy. Kind of tall."

"But not a racist like his father?"

"He actually commented on that," Celeste said. "He's aware that Irwin has those biases."

"Yet he works for the guy."

Celeste shrugged. "Family is complicated."

"Are you going to sleep with him?"

"I'm not sure. He's hot, but it might not be

wise. Not just because of the case—I'm not sure I want to get embroiled with that kind of guy."

"You just said he was hot."

"There's more to it than that. He's a scion with a corner office, and his company's business model is built on corruption."

"At least he's honest about his father's stupidity."

"I haven't been honest with him, though. He thinks my name is Penelope."

Truman laughed. "That never stopped you before."

Celeste drained her glass. "I wish I could offer you a ride, but I'm on the metro."

"It's not that late. I'll be fine to walk."

She gathered up her change, leaving some singles for the bartender, and followed Truman down the stairs.

"I'll pick you up at eight," she said, and headed for the station.

Walking home on the fringes of Skid Row, Truman felt light, and not just from the tequila. Dyson was still alive. But why had he disappeared, and why was he in league with Jeffries?

Someone across the street shouted, and Truman looked over. It wasn't about him, as no one was in sight. The voice had emanated from one of the tents along the sidewalk. Dyson wanted to help these people, and worked on it every day.

Why would he help a rich asshole who built fortresses for other rich folks that excluded these people? The most likely possibility was bleak—he'd taken a payoff. That's how Jeffries handled bureaucrats and politicians, and Truman knew as well as anyone how intoxicating money was.

Once he was up in his loft, he peeled off his clothes and killed the lights, then climbed into bed with Biff Sturgis, reading by the light of the bedside lamp. Everyone had contradictions, he knew that, but Dyson's seemed so extreme. In the index, he found an entry for "consistency," and flipped to the page:

> Don't expect consistency from anybody—crooks, cops, dames, even judges. The same sap who puts in a pious performance on Sunday morning was high as a kite in a gin joint on Saturday night. The granny with the impeccable Gilded Age manners in springtime will lunge for your eye with a hat pin once the heat of summer sets in. When the Santanas blow, that sweet cashier at the soda fountain might just carve you up with her boning knife and wrap the pieces in butcher paper and twine.

It was a reasonable insight, but more interesting was mention of the Santanas—Biff had to mean the Santa Anas, the hot dusty wind that sometimes blew down from the desert. The only place they were called that was here. Truman checked the front of the book. It had been published in New York, but Biff had clearly been an Angeleno. He hadn't picked up on that before. It seemed even more appropriate now that Truman was gradually acquiring his wisdom.

FOURTEEN

Waking early to the alarm on his phone, Truman slapped it off and crawled out of bed. Once he got the espresso machine working, he went to the bathroom and splashed water on his face. He'd only had one drink last night, but the skin under his eyes looked dark. At this rate he'd soon look like his homeless neighbors—all he needed now was to grow out his beard.

He went across the room to flick through his clothes rack. The rust-red pants, he decided. Not for the color, but because they were lightweight, and it was supposed to be warm today.

It was odd to be up this early. Standing in the middle of the room, he sipped his espresso and turned his face to the windows to let the bright light sink in and spark wakefulness. Celeste wasn't due for a while, so he slammed his coffee and went to the fridge to retrieve a cucumber, then cut several thin slices from it. Sprawling on the sofa, he closed his eyes and applied the cool rounds to his eyelids and the dark patches of skin.

Truman started awake when the door buzzer sounded. When he answered, a staticky voice said "ee," probably originally "It's me," but he recognized Celeste's voice. He buzzed her in, then unlocked the door and munched on the cucumber slices. When Celeste stepped in, she was dressed for the office again, in black trousers and a gray houndstooth blouse.

"You look great," Truman said.

"And you have a cucumber slice on your face."

He felt for it, and peeled it off, and offered it to her.

"No thanks," she said, wrinkling her nose.

"Angel and Beretta kept calling me Sunshine," he said, and took a bite of it. "So I thought I'd stop moisturizing, to toughen up my look. But then I realized I can have great skin and still be tough."

Celeste furrowed her brow. "That sounds like a real breakthrough."

"Want an espresso?"

"I'd love one," she said, and went over to drop onto the purple sofa.

"So what's Blanca like?" Truman called to her, as he tapped the used grounds into the garbage.

"A little younger than me. She likes to go clubbing."

"I mean her worldview—is she the play-by-the-rules type, or the get-it-done type?"

"She's not in the thrall of the man, but we should definitely have a story that sounds better than we're stalking someone."

Truman stepped over to hand her a steaming little demitasse cup, then sat on the adjacent sofa.

"We can tell her that it's my phone," he said, "and I misplaced it, but I don't have a tracking app installed."

"Perfect. We can show her the receipt to really sell it."

"It doesn't have my name on it, though."

"But you work for Irwin Jeffries, and it's your company cell phone. How embarrassing that you misplaced it."

"Right," Truman said, grinning at her. "I'm afraid to tell me boss. Who wouldn't sympathize with that?"

When Celeste had finished her cup, she rose. "We should go."

Truman followed her down to the street, and glanced into the alley as they climbed into the little blue car. There was no sign of life, just the tops of the tents in the shadow of the adjacent building. Celeste drove to the Financial District and had to circle the block a couple of times before she found an open street space. While she drove, Truman pulled up the receipt that Celeste had photographed and spent a minute memorizing the phone number. After they got out and Celeste fed the meter, they walked around the corner to the cell phone store.

It was a small place, fronting the busy sidewalk, with two staffers behind the counter. The man was occupied with a customer, and the woman smiled in recognition when they stepped inside. There was some family resemblance, Truman decided, although Blanca wasn't quite as tall as Celeste, and she wore her hair short.

"This is my friend Truman," Celeste said, as they approached the counter.

Blanca acknowledged him, then said to her, "How are you, girl?"

The pair of them gossiped for a minute about relatives, and then Celeste shifted gears.

"So—Truman lost his phone."

"You need a new one?" Blanca said, eyeing him. "I can set you up."

"We were hoping you could track it," Celeste said, "and tell him where he left it."

She raised her eyebrows. "Are you trying to get me fired?"

"I have the receipt," Truman said. "My

company paid for it, and I don't want to get in trouble with them if I don't have to."

"He's such an airhead," Celeste said, ignoring Truman as he shot her a look.

"I can see that," Blanca said grimly, then turned to her computer screen. "What's the number?"

Truman recited it, glad that it had stuck in his memory, as Blanca tapped at the keyboard.

Staring at the screen, Blanca's eyes narrowed. "Irwin Jeffries?"

"That's my boss," Truman said.

"So you've been in Palm Springs."

He felt his heart start to pound. "That's right."

"It looks like the phone is still at your hotel. It's switched on."

"Which hotel?" Truman said. When Blanca eyed him, he shrugged. "I stayed at several."

"He's kind of slutty," Celeste offered.

"Smuggler's Glade."

"That is such a relief," Truman said. "You may have saved my job."

"Not a word about this to anyone," Blanca said, looking from him to Celeste.

"It's already forgotten." Celeste leaned across the counter to give her an air kiss. "Ciao, *chica*."

Once they were out on the street, walking back to the car, Truman said, "I know that place. It's a nudie boys hotel. If Dyson is hanging out there, he's a skank."

"Not that you're in any position to judge him. You're just upset that he didn't instantly want to be exclusive with you."

Truman sighed. "That may be part of it."

"So what's the plan now?"

"I'll drive out there and talk to him. Maybe I'll find out what's going on. Do you want to come with?"

"I want to take another crack at getting into Irwin's computer," she said, "and maybe grill Flint."

"Is there any point now? We already know where Dyson is."

"Think beyond your libido. Don't you want to know whether Jeffries bribed the bureaucrats to eliminate the transitional housing from his stupid condo tower? Maybe find out how he's using his wealth to bend the rules?"

"That would be interesting material," Truman said, "but then what do we do with it?"

"I'm not sure. At the very least, we could pass it on to a few journalists."

"That's probably the most we can do." As they walked up to Celeste's car, he added, "Can I borrow your wheels?"

Celeste knew he was going to ask. She dug the key out of her pocket. "Be gentle. And bring it back gassed up."

"Can I drop you at Jeffries's office?"

"It's two blocks. I'll walk." She watched as Truman stepped around to the driver's door. "Keep it under eighty on the freeway."

Once he'd climbed in and waved good-bye, Truman spent a minute adjusting the seats and the mirrors and finding his radio station. Easing into the traffic, he headed toward the freeway.

He didn't drive very often, so he had to focus intently at first, but soon he got used to it and was cruising along comfortably. The 10 wasn't all that congested at this hour, and it felt good to be on the road, to see more of the sky. The little car rode loud but it went fast, and he cranked up the music until he lost the signal somewhere past Redlands.

Driving into the Coachella Valley, the freeway wound through a forest of lazily rotating wind turbines. It always took a while to get used to the desert landscape. The air was so dry that things looked sharper, more vivid, closer than they really were.

Once he was in the town, he rolled down the windows. It was hot but not yet that insane blistering summer heat that kept people indoors all day. He was glad he'd worn the light pants.

The navigation on his phone led him to Smugglers Glade, and soon he was pulling into the parking lot. He left Celeste's car under a sun shade and walked into the reception area. It was abandoned save for the guy behind the counter, who was in his sixties and wore a brown rug that ended abruptly at his temples, exposing the gray of his sideburns.

"Can I buy a day pass for the pool?" Truman asked him.

"Sure thing," the guy said, casually looking him over. "You know it's clothing-optional?"

"That's why I'm here."

He grinned and turned to grab a towel and a key attached to a wrist strap as Truman pulled out some cash.

"The locker room is through there," he said, gesturing with his chin as he pawed at the register to make change. "The pool deck is beyond that. Just leave the key in the locker door when you're done with it."

Truman went into the locker room and found the box with his key number. He put the key in the lock but didn't bother to get undressed, instead draping the towel around his shoulders, over his shirt, and walked out to the deck.

A couple of billowing canvas cabanas were set up at one side, and potted banana palms dotted the deck. The water looked cool and inviting. In the shade at the far end was a bar. There were just a few guys around, most of them naked, sprawled on loungers. A couple of them were floating languorously on inflatable mats in the pool and chatting in subdued tones. Despite all the exposed flesh, it didn't feel erotic at all.

He spotted Dyson almost right away. Palm Springs was pretty white, especially the gay part, and Dyson stood out as the lone black guy. It really was him, he saw, walking around the pool. Dyson was still alive. What a relief. He was stretched out on a lounger in the shade, with mirrored sunglasses on, a towel under his head. His eyes must be closed, Truman realized, as Dyson didn't react as he strode toward him. Truman was feeling relief, he realized, but also a little anger at the anguish Dyson had caused for Ivy and Bug. He could feel a surge of adrenaline well up as he got closer.

———◆———

On the elevator ride up to Jeffries's office, Celeste tied her hair back and put on the red-framed glasses from the breast pocket of her shirt. When she walked in, Reggie looked up and scowled.

"Where have you been?"

"Is he looking for me?"

"He's not in yet, but you're very late."

Celeste smiled and shrugged as she walked by. "Traffic."

If Jeffries was expected, she couldn't very well go in and try to break into his computer. In Martina's office, she spent some time messing around on her computer, trying to dig deeper into the files on the servers. Some of the folders looked like they might contain financial data, but they weren't accessible, and there wasn't any explanation why. Eventually she got frustrated and gave up. She wasn't going to learn anything here about what happened with the money.

Looking at Jeffries's calendar, there was nothing listed for today, but tomorrow evening, two hours were blocked off as "Personal." There were no details, as it was one of the blank events synced from his private calendar, to block out the time so that Martina wouldn't double-book him.

The Provigil she'd taken earlier wasn't making the day go any faster, but it was making her feel impatient. Maybe she should have taken more than half a tab. She was startled out of her thoughts when the door to the inner office flew open. Jeffries stood in the doorway, wearing the same drab green suit he'd had on yesterday.

"I need you to get me Stroud on the phone," Jeffries said.

"Of course," Celeste said. "Is that a company?"

Jeffries scowled. "It's a man's name, dummy. He works for me. He's not picking up. Get him out of the shower if you have to. I need to talk to him."

He pulled the door closed as he stepped back into his office.

There was a company directory somewhere, Celeste remembered, and clicking around, soon brought it up. There was an entry for a man named Michael Stroud, accompanied by a photo. He had blond hair and cherubic cheeks, grinning at the camera, and like everyone who worked here above the level of the clerks and cleaners, he was Anglo.

She dialed Stroud's work number and got a voice-mail message. Next she dialed the cell number listed for him, and it went to voice mail too. No home number was listed, but there was a home address, in Culver City. Of course people like Stroud lived over there. It was disproportionately white, as it used to be a sundown town, where nonwhites were rounded up and arrested if they lingered after dark.

A web search for his home address brought up a list of real estate agents that contained a different name, Marilyn Stroud, and a new phone number. When she dialed, a woman's voice answered.

"Irwin Jeffries calling for Michael Stroud," Celeste said.

"Oh, god. Are you kidding me? He's taking a personal day."

"Mr. Jeffries needs to speak with him as soon as possible."

She huffed and said, "Just a second."

"This is Michael," a man's voice said.

"Please hold for Irwin Jeffries."

Celeste tapped the hold button and replaced the receiver, then stepped into Jeffries's office. He was hunched over his desk, gazing at the computer screen, and briefly glanced up.

"What is it, sugar?"

"I have Michael Stroud on the phone."

Jeffries sat up and eyed her. "Finally." He picked up the receiver and raised his voice. "Stroud, you asshole, did you have a stroke? I'm looking at this paperwork ..."

Celeste didn't hear the rest of it, as she closed the door behind her. No wonder Martina had been so willing to cede this desk for a few days.

Glancing at the office directory again, she found Flint's extension and dialed. When he picked up, she said, "Where's your office?"

"Penelope? It's farther down the hall, past the kitchen. The door at the end. It has a plaque on it that says 'Flint Jeffries.'"

She hung up and strode through reception, ignoring Reggie. At Flint's door she knocked and then pushed her way in. He was alone at his desk, facing the windows that filled two of the walls, like Irwin's. The view was toward Hollywood and the hazy hills rising beyond.

"Sweet corner office," Celeste said, looking around. "It's almost as big as your dad's."

"I guess that's a perk of having his last name." Flint reclined in his chair, lacing his fingers behind his head. "I had fun last night."

"Me too. Listen, today's my last day. Do you want to have dinner with me?"

"Very much," he said, and sat up.

"Good answer. Pick me up on your way out."

She walked out and went back to Martina's desk. There was a text from Saffron, she saw, checking her phone:

Call me.

"You did it," Saffron said when she picked up.

"It sounds like whatever I did was a good thing."

"You sold *Lemon Study 4*."

"That's great news."

"That buyer couldn't get hold of you, and he started to think you were going to sell it to someone else. He got so worried that he came in and bought four pieces from the exhibition."

"That's huge," Celeste said. "I can't believe he did that."

"Scarcity is a motivator, darling."

"Well, I won't be sorry to see it go."

"When are you coming back to me?"

"Tomorrow, or maybe Sunday."

"Very well," Saffron said. "And congratulations."

As she hung up, Celeste had to smile. That was indeed good news. On her phone, she found her earlier exchange with Martina, and sent her a text:

> I'm done here. You can wind up your family emergency.

Her reply came a moment later:

> Did you learn anything?

Celeste thumb-typed a response:

> Not sure yet.

FIFTEEN

Walking past the swimming pool, Truman sat sideways on the lounger adjacent to Dyson's.

"Nice to see that you're alive," he said.

Dyson's body jerked like he'd been shocked. He sat up and raised his sunglasses.

"What are you doing here?"

"Your sister thinks you're dead."

His face contorted in a scowl. "What?"

Dyson reached for his towel and draped it over his crotch, like demure medieval Venus with her red hair.

"I've seen your junk before," Truman said.

"I told Ivy what I was doing. That I was going away for a few days."

"You also told her you were thinking of

extorting Irwin Jeffries."

"Why were you talking to Ivy?" His brow furrowed. "And how did you find me?"

"Never mind all that. Why are you out here on Irwin Jeffries's dime?"

He eyed Truman for a moment. "You're very good at your job."

"I know that," Truman said, raising his voice. "Now sing, brother."

Dyson's eyes flicked to the other men around the pool. He spoke quietly. "Did Ivy tell you what was on the memory card?"

"I know you have something that might embarrass Jeffries."

"It's a set of about a dozen photos of him living it up at a neo-Nazi rally."

Truman nodded, relieved that his story jibed with Ivy's. It meant it was more likely to be the truth.

"What did you do with the negatives?"

"You already know about this," Dyson said, his brow furrowing. "How much did Ivy tell you?"

"As much as she knows, I think. Did you destroy the negatives?"

"They're in a place where no one will ever find them."

"And you're sure that you're the only one who has the images."

"They were originals. I doubt they were ever

printed. That's why I tried to sell them to Jeffries."

"We call that blackmail," Truman said flatly. "How did he react?"

"It got his attention. I emailed him part of one photo, with just his head, and the collar of his brown shirt, and the pine trees behind him. I cropped out the Nazi stuff, but I knew he'd realize what it was."

"Did you meet with him?"

"At a restaurant." He waved a hand. "I figured I'd be safe in a public place."

Truman's gaze dropped to Dyson's perfect pecs. Celeste was right—it was hard to stay objective when he was attracted to the guy. But right now he needed to stay focused.

"You gave him the memory card?" Truman said.

"I didn't even take it with me," Dyson said. "We hadn't discussed terms yet. We sat at a table in a dark corner and just talked. Jeffries remembered me as one of the people who spoke out at meetings and wrote letters to the planning department about his condo tower. I reminded him that it wasn't just me. Lots of Skid Row stakeholders spoke out. All we really wanted was for him to keep his word, and provide a percentage as transitional housing."

"Plus some cash for you personally," Truman said. "For those photos."

Dyson sighed and looked toward the pool.

"You're conflating two different issues," Truman went on. "It seems that Jeffries has pretty much weaseled out of the low-income housing thing."

"I guess we knew all along that he would."

"Why did Jeffries give you a phone and a credit card?"

"He wanted me out of town for a couple of days," Dyson said. "If I didn't agree to disappear, he said he'd make my life difficult, and have me roughed up. I puffed out my chest and told him that I still had the photos from Oregon, so I was the one calling the shots. But he's a hard-ass. You can't play tough with a guy like that."

"So he bullied you into taking a poolside vacation with a bunch of hot guys," Truman said.

"Jeffries didn't pick this place. He made it easy—the credit card was so that I could go wherever I wanted. I thought that was safer. Less likely that he'll come after me to rough me up."

"If that was his plan, he would have done it already. Why did he give you a phone?"

"I'm supposed to be incommunicado for a few days. The deal was that I wouldn't turn on my own phone, not that I wouldn't look at any screen. A boy needs to keep up with the world."

"It has to be about A Cut Above," Truman said. "He didn't want you communicating with your Skid Row people."

"I'm sure you think I'm a coward," Dyson said quietly. "That I knuckled under to a bully."

"I'm not here to judge you. When are you supposed to go back?"

"Jeffries said the day after tomorrow."

"That means he's up to something before that," Truman said. "Why does he want you personally out of the picture? There are other people who speak out against the condo project."

"He did ask me how I always got wind that he'd had a private meeting with city staff, and how I got the details so quickly about the changes he'd negotiated."

"How do you?"

"I have a source at city hall," Dyson said. "I always share the leaks with other activists, so I didn't think it would be that obvious that it started with me."

"Did you tell Jeffries about that?"

"I didn't want to endanger my source, so I hedged."

"Can you put me in contact with this person?"

Dyson slowly shook his head. "It's a personal connection. He'd freak out. No matter how I framed it, he wouldn't talk to you."

"So Jeffries suspects that you have a source," Truman said. "That's why you're here. He can't identify the leak, but he can achieve the same result by silencing you for a while."

He sighed. "He's probably got a meeting planned with the city bureaucrats."

"More than one," Truman said slowly. "There was a block of time reserved in his calendar for Wednesday evening, so he got you to leave the day before. And you're not supposed to come back until Sunday—something is going down this weekend."

"How do you know what's in his calendar?"

"You said it yourself," Truman said, waving his arm. "I'm good at what I do. So a meeting with the bureaucrats—what would that look like?"

"More payoffs to rubber-stamp changes to A Cut Above. Probably to make it even more exclusive—a moat full of alligators, or a laser death ray on the roof. Whatever the result, the meeting will be clandestine. No agenda, no minutes, no record of it."

"Does your source leak to anyone else?"

"I don't think so. Jeffries obviously pinpointed me as the recipient."

Truman watched him for a moment, thinking it through.

"Do you want me to come back with you?" Dyson said.

"Dance with the one that brung you."

He frowned. "What?"

"Jeffries gave you money—you should stick

to the deal you made with him. Otherwise he probably will have you roughed up. What did he say about the neo-Nazi photos?"

"That he was too busy, and we'd deal with it when I got back."

"It sounds like he doesn't care," Truman said. "Maybe he thinks it won't hurt him."

"It got me a meeting, though. I think that means he's going to try to buy them."

Truman took a deep breath. "I want you to give me that memory card."

"Why would I do that," Dyson said, cocking his head, "when there's money to be made?"

"Two reasons. One, you should be ashamed of yourself for enabling Irwin Jeffries."

Dyson frowned. "You said you weren't here to judge me."

"I changed my mind," Truman said flatly. "You're one of the good ones, Dyson, with that job of yours, and the activism. I know you're trying to make the world better."

"Don't put that on me. I have to take care of myself first."

Truman threw up his hands. "That relates to the second reason. Have you heard of the black-mailer's ultimate reward?"

He frowned. "Cash?"

"It means you're going to wind up in a shallow grave up in the Angeles National Forest with a bullet in your skull. Jeffries just hasn't done it yet because you were so easy to manipulate."

Dyson turned to look at the guys in the pool, where the sun glinted off the ripples in the water. "So you're not just going to sell the photos to Jeffries yourself?"

"Of course not. Then I'd be the dead guy."

"I know you're right," he said, not meeting Truman's gaze. "I can feel it. The whole blackmail thing wasn't even my idea."

Truman waved his arm. "I know it wasn't Ivy's."

"My roommate Bug thought we could make some quick cash."

"I met that guy. He's not really what I'd call firmly grounded in reality, or even rational."

"Why did you talk to Bug?"

"Because he thought you were already dead."

Dyson winced and looked away. Truman waited, as he could see the wheels turning, and watched him absently stroke the arm of the lounger.

"Come up to my room," he said finally.

Dyson wrapped his towel around his shoulders, and scooped up the little canvas bag beside his lounger. Truman followed him through a set of glass doors and into the stairwell, admiring his athletic butt. A naked guy with a heavy tan was making his way down the stairs, and eyed

Truman as he passed. The meaning in his intent gaze was unmistakable.

"It's easy to get laid in this place, huh," Truman said, once they were upstairs.

"That's why we're all here."

Dyson unlocked his room with a key card from his bag, then made sure the door was closed after Truman stepped in. It was surprisingly spacious, with a king bed and windows onto the pool deck.

Truman watched as Dyson stepped over to the bureau and squatted in front of it, then pulled out a drawer and reached underneath. He felt around and pulled off a strip of clear tape. It had a little black rectangle in the middle—the memory card. Once he'd folded the sticky part of the tape onto itself, he handed it to Truman.

"I know you're trying to save me from myself," Dyson said, "but what are you going to do with it? Destroy it?"

Truman tucked it into his hip pocket. "I haven't figured that out yet. But I won't be selling it to Irwin Jeffries." Studying his face, he realized Dyson looked a little forlorn. "You're doing the right thing."

"I know that. It doesn't mean it feels good." Dyson sighed, then nodded toward the bed. "Want to mess around?"

"I can't," Truman said carefully. "I'm going

back to LA. You should call your sister."

"The deal with Jeffries was no communication."

"I'll talk to her, then."

"Don't tell her where I am, or why. I'll handle all that later."

Truman nodded, and Dyson stepped closer, reaching up to caress his cheek.

"You're kind of a hard-ass. I didn't see that before."

"Sometimes I have to be."

"I also know that you're a good person."

"I think we all are," Truman said. "Most of the time, anyway."

He squeezed Dyson's hand, and lingered for a moment, then went to the door, not looking back as he stepped out and headed for the stairs.

Once he was in the car, he started the engine to get the air conditioner blowing, then texted Ivy:

> I just met with Dyson. He's fine. He'll call you on Sunday. I can't answer any questions, so don't even ask.

She'd respond soon, he knew, and put on his seatbelt, then sat there with the engine idling while he waited, phone in his palm, gazing out at a couple of well-coiffed guys walking across the parking lot toward an SUV. When his phone rang, he picked up without even checking to see who it was.

"Where did you find him?" Ivy demanded.

"I can't tell you that. He'll explain it himself on Sunday."

"I'm just so relieved. Is he healthy? He's not being held against his will?"

"Dyson is safe and self-determined."

"So why can't you talk about it? Jeffries didn't get to you, did he?"

"Of course not," Truman said flatly. "It's not my place to gossip about what Dyson is doing. He thought that leaving those messages the other night meant that nobody would be worried. It surprised him that they'd had the opposite effect."

Ivy sighed. "I wish you'd tell me what's going on."

"Dyson will tell you himself. For now, I'd be relieved that he's OK. Can you let Bug know?"

"If I don't hear from Dyson on Sunday, I'm going to sic the cops on you."

"If you don't hear from him by then, call me. I'll tell you everything I know."

After he ended the call, Truman pulled up the navigation app and put his phone in the dash mount, then drove out of the parking lot and headed toward the freeway. Once he was on the open road, he called Celeste, glad that she picked up, and told her what he'd learned.

"Dyson must be really scared," Celeste said,

"if he voluntarily switched off his phone for a week. It would take a lot to get me to do that."

"Jeffries gave him that other phone to play with, and the hotel he's in is pretty cushy. I just wish I could talk to his source at city hall to find out what Jeffries is up to this weekend."

"Maybe I can find out. I'm having dinner with a Jeffries in a few hours."

"Flint," Truman said, lowering his voice. "You think he'd rat out his own father?"

"He might."

"That would be amazing. Call me after."

"I can hear a lot of road noise," Celeste said. "Slow down—don't wreck my car."

"It's just straining a little to get out of the Coachella Valley. A few more miles and then it's all downhill."

SIXTEEN

Celeste had her feet on the desk, reading art-world news on her phone. Eyeing the clock, she saw that it was pushing six. It was hard to believe these people were still working so late on a Friday evening.

Finally Flint appeared, stepping in from the hall. He was wearing his suit jacket now, cobalt blue and sleek, in a coarse silk fabric. The man knew how to dress.

"You look comfortable," he said.

"While the boss is away," Celeste said, and swung her feet off the desk. "I think Irwin left already."

"I love those shoes."

The chunky black flats weren't that special, she knew, and she wore them because they were comfortable to walk in. But a compliment was a compliment.

"A homeless woman accused me of stealing them from her the other day."

Flint laughed. "Are you ready to go?"

"Where are we eating?" she said, rising and gathering up her bag.

"You can pick."

She walked with him into the hall, then out to the reception area, where Reggie's desk sat abandoned. Flint followed Celeste into the elevator lobby.

"How far out of your comfort zone are you willing to go?" she said.

"No food trucks."

She chuckled at that. "We can find a place with tables and chairs."

"Not the central market. That place gets way too busy on a Friday night."

"There's a Mexican place on Seventh. The food is decent."

It was close enough to walk, and soon they were out on the street in the waning daylight. The sidewalks were busy with commuters. As they stepped past a guy who was shuffling along the curb, gesturing absently, muttering to himself, Flint put a protective hand around her shoulder. The guy didn't look dangerous, and even if he was, Celeste could have handled him on her own. But it was a sweet gesture.

They got seated and ordered food, and Celeste had to smile when Flint asked the waiter his name.

"You like to connect with people," she said, once they were alone again.

"It's selfish, in a way. It makes me feel good."

"So why do you work for your father?"

"I'm learning the business. The plan is that I'll eventually take over."

"I thought you had shareholders. Don't they decide things like that?"

"The company's not really publicly traded. There are a few investors, but the majority of it is still held by the family."

Celeste nodded. "I know you don't share your father's values. Do you plan to do things differently once you're in charge?"

"Of course. People in this town think Irwin is some kind of cartoon villain. It's a reasonable assessment—he acts like one. In business you always make enemies, but I know it's possible to be more ethical than he is."

"How soon until you're the boss? Irwin must be in his seventies."

"He's the same generation as the hippies," Flint said, "but he didn't adopt their thinking. He went to the other extreme. I always wondered what my life would have been like if he'd been different. Who would I be if Irwin had been part of the counterculture?"

"You could have been born in the back of a van."

Flint chuckled. "That's how it happened in the sixties. I was born in the eighties. The hippies weren't nomads anymore, but they weren't like Irwin either."

The food arrived, and they tucked into it.

"I love this," Flint said, waving a forkful of mole-drenched masa. "You've given me a new place for my repertoire."

After she'd eaten part of her own meal, Celeste set her fork aside.

"So you know Irwin is a dinosaur," she said, "and he's on the wrong side of history."

"Sure."

"What is he doing this weekend that's so secret?"

Flint frowned and eyed her warily. "Are you one of those Skid Row activists?"

"I'm not, but I have to live in this city with everyone else. Your father has a knack for building things that alienate people, and widen class divisions, and make life worse for most of us."

"Ouch."

"You know it's true."

"I'm not denying it," Flint said. "But why do you want to know what he's up to this weekend?

Did you infiltrate my office to gather intel? Are you wining and dining me to extract information?"

Celeste chuckled and waved a hand. "I'm an office temp, not a Cold War spy. And you're the one who invited me out, remember? I'm asking because Irwin bullied someone I know into leaving town for a few days. Do you know anything about that?"

Flint's eyebrows shot up. "Who?"

"A friend of a friend. He's one of Irwin's critics."

He gestured with his fork. "So he's the activist. Are you planning on telling him what Irwin's doing so he can picket and shout at him with a megaphone?"

"This guy is too afraid to come back. Irwin used the threat of violence to make sure he stayed out of town until Sunday."

"I know he's unethical, but Irwin wouldn't hurt anyone."

"But he did threaten to."

Flint looked down at his plate. "I hate the way Irwin acts sometimes."

He wasn't questioning the veracity of her story, Celeste realized. He knew what Irwin was capable of.

"This guy works on Skid Row," Celeste said, "so it has to be about A Cut Above. Irwin's calendar has a block of private time tomorrow evening at seven. Could that be something that he wants to keep secret from the Skid Row stakeholders?"

"Penelope, think about it—you're asking me to sabotage my own company."

"Or is it improving your company? Why not start the cleanup now, rather than biding your time to get into the big office?"

Flint scoffed. "Irwin would be very angry."

"It seems to me that he's always angry. And he won't be angry with you—he won't know where the tip came from."

"Say I find out what's on his agenda. What are you going to do with that information?"

She sighed. "I don't know, exactly. Maybe some of the other Skid Row people will show up with a megaphone, like you said, and embarrass him."

"That's no easy task. The man has no shame."

"I'm thinking the secrecy is because he's going to be schmoozing with bureaucrats. At the very least, if he's meeting public employees, that should be public knowledge. You know the saying that sunlight is a great disinfectant? Get it out in the open. If it's just Irwin playing golf with his cronies or getting his back waxed, no one is going to care."

"If you interfere with his dealings, it could be bad for me, and bad for my business."

"But illuminating Irwin's dirty tricks might be beneficial in the long run. Maybe it would bring down some corrupt bureaucrats, or at least discourage them from wallowing in the sleaze. I'm sure it doesn't seem like it now, but that kind of corruption will eventually come back to bite you in the ass. In your business, sweeping it away could even give you a chance to exert more control, and nudge Irwin toward better practices. What's the worst thing that could happen? Instead of millions and millions and millions, you'll make millions and millions."

"You really don't know how business works," Flint said. A smile played on his lips. "If the choice is between morals and millions, the answer is always going to be millions."

"Fine," Celeste said, and waved a hand. "But you don't have to become your father."

Flint watched her for a moment. "Do you know about the most recent compromise we made on A Cut Above?"

"It's going to be two buildings, to physically separate the rich and the poor."

"That's old news. Irwin got the city to agree to zero transitional housing. In exchange there'll be some low-income units and a park. The thing he didn't publicize is that the park will be for residents only."

"So it's not really a park," Celeste said. "It's a private yard."

"Correct. And like always, in the end there

won't be any low-income units built."

"The Skid Row people say he achieves all that by bribing the planning and zoning people."

"And the politicians," Flint said, reaching for his water glass. "Allegedly. I've never seen it happen."

"You're smart not to know anything about it. It's called plausible deniability."

"If he scared your friend off for the weekend, I'm thinking you're right, he's planned a meeting with the bureaucrats. What did his calendar say?"

"The only event listed before Monday is tomorrow evening," Celeste said, leaning toward him. "It would be great if you could find out who he's meeting, and where."

"You know, it's extremely difficult to say no to a beautiful woman."

"Don't do it for me," she said, and frowned. "Do it to clean up your company's karma."

Flint pulled his phone from his inside pocket and tapped at it, then set it on the table and put a finger to his lips. Celeste could hear it ringing—he'd put the call on speaker.

Irwin's tinny voice answered. "What do you need?"

"Hey, dad," Flint said. "Do you have time for dinner tomorrow night?"

"I've got a meeting."

"About the concrete?"

"It's with the idiots from the city. It should be the last time I have to grease the wheels on A Cut Above. I want to get that fucker built."

"Are you taking them for steak?" Flint said.

"Does it matter?" Irwin demanded. "Why do you need to see me tomorrow?"

"It's nothing urgent. Call me when you have some free time."

Irwin scoffed audibly and hung up. Flint scooped up the phone and tucked it into his jacket.

"If my father talked to me like that," Celeste said, "I'd stop paying rent."

Flint frowned. "You pay your father rent?"

"It's well below market rate." She waved dismissively. "So Irwin is meeting bureaucrats, but he didn't say where."

"I know where. He takes them to a steak house on Fig. They keep it dark inside, so you can't see the rats, or the bales of cash that the rats take."

"He actually does that?" Celeste said. "Hands out cash?"

"It's a metaphor. The restaurant has a private room in the back. He invites a group of them to win everyone over at the same time. If he can get them all on board together, with the group mentality, it's less likely that any individual will balk or back out."

"I assume 'win over' is a euphemism for 'bribe.'"

"You heard none of this from me," Flint said. He waved at the waiter and mouthed "Check."

After he'd paid, they went out into the cool evening air.

"Would you like to come to my place for a drink?" Flint said, facing her on the sidewalk and sliding his hands into his pockets.

"I'd love that," Celeste said, "but then I wouldn't want to leave. I've got stuff to do."

"I probably don't want to know about that."

"Smart man. Maintain your plausible deniability."

He flashed a sad smile. "Am I going to see you again?"

"I want to. Right now things are too hot. I'll call you in a week or so, when nobody at your office remembers my face."

"Are you sure you're not a spy?"

"If I were, I would have come home with you last night and bugged your apartment."

Flint chuckled. "Are you going to kiss me, at least?"

Celeste reached for his neck and gently pulled him closer, meeting his mouth and spending a minute lost in it. He ran his hands down her back, and leaned into her. Eventually she pulled back.

"To be continued," she said.

"I'll take that as a promise."

Celeste turned away, and walked toward the metro station, her heart fluttering from the intensity of the connection, the warmth of his skin. Stopping at the corner to wait for the crossing light, she pulled out her phone and called Truman.

When he picked up, she said, "Are you still on the road?"

"There's so much traffic on Friday," he wailed. "I'm finally coming up on Union Station."

"Are you on the 101? Get off at Spring Street." Celeste turned around, retracing her steps. "I'll be walking north from Seventh."

Twilight was deepening as she turned onto Spring, and most of the drivers had their headlights on. She watched the stream of traffic as she walked. Before long the familiar grill of her car appeared, and she waved her arm. Truman pulled up to the curb, and put on the flashers, and climbed out.

"Can you drive?" he said. "I'm so not used to it. It took three hours to get here, and that's just from San Berdoo, where the traffic started."

"You look like you've run a marathon," she said, and stepped around to the driver's side.

"I feel like I got trampled by a marathon."

Truman climbed in the passenger's seat, and Celeste adjusted the mirrors before she pulled out.

"Do you want to get a drink somewhere?" she said.

"Let's go to my place—I'm exhausted. I'm going to order some food." He tapped at his phone. "Do you want some spring rolls?"

"I just ate," Celeste said, checking the side mirror to change lanes. "With Flint. He kind of opened up tonight."

"About his painful childhood?"

"About our case, you ninny."

"Really? What did he say?"

Celeste told him about their conversation, and about Flint's phone call to his father.

"I wonder why he let you listen in?" Truman said.

"It's a way to be completely transparent. I didn't get a secondhand account about what Irwin told him—he wanted me to hear it myself."

"Excellent detective work," Truman said. "It sounds like Irwin's meeting tomorrow is the final installment of the bribery payments."

"That's the implication, although Flint said he's never actually seen it happening. But he knows it happens."

"What did he know about Dyson?"

"Nothing, but he wasn't surprised that Jeffries scared him into disappearing for a few days."

Truman was quiet for a moment. "Why would Flint rat out his father? He knows the guy is a creep, but they're in business together."

"I played the 'do the right thing' card. He wants to steer the company in a better direction."

"I guess that's plausible. Are we sure it's not a trap?"

"He's not that guy," Celeste said, braking for a red light and eyeing him sidelong.

"Is that an objective assessment? I mean, did you sleep with him?"

"No," she snapped. "At least not yet."

Celeste parked in front of his building, and they climbed out. Truman winced and arched his back.

"That was a lot of driving for you," she said.

"Plus it's so dry out there. I drank a ton of water on the way home."

Following him inside, Celeste had to grin. She knew exactly where the empties would be— right where he tossed them, in her backseat.

"I want to change clothes," Truman said, stepping into his loft.

Celeste went over to the sofas and stretched out on the purple one. A minute later the buzzer for the front door sounded.

"That's my food," Truman called from the bathroom. "Can you go? Tip the guy a few bucks. They hate coming here."

Celeste got up, and trotted down to the front door, and handed the guy a fin in exchange for the white plastic bag. When she got back upstairs, Truman had changed into a pair of gym shorts and a T-shirt. She handed him the food, and sat on the adjacent sofa as he pulled it out of the bag. After he wolfed down the order of spring rolls, he started on the noodles at a more leisurely pace.

Between bites, he said, "I think I know why Flint was down with throwing his father under the bus."

"He knows Irwin is a dick," Celeste said, "and that he treats people like trash. That's why Martina was willing to flip on him too."

"Or," Truman said, holding her gaze, "Flint wants to oust him, and take control of the company. You've given him fuel for a coup d'état."

Celeste thought about it. "That's definitely a darker spin on it. I guess it's possible. The only privileged information Flint gave me, though, was about the meeting tomorrow. He thinks we're going to interrupt it with a protest. Flint knows that's not going to bring down Irwin Jeffries."

"So what are we going to do?" Truman said, his mouth half full of noodles.

"What are our options?"

"I got the neo-Nazi photos from Dyson."

Celeste frowned. "Why would he give them to you?"

"I told him he'd wind up dead if he tried to extort Irwin Jeffries. Dyson believed me. They just had the one meeting, but the guy really must have intimidated him."

"So Irwin used the carrot and the stick." She chuckled. "Get out of town, punk, but here, use my credit card while you're away."

"I'm not even sure how much of it is true. You found the evidence for the carrot part, but when it comes to the threats, all I have is Dyson's word."

"He definitely lied to you about other stuff."

Truman sighed. "I think I need to be done with that guy."

"You mean no more hookups, or that he's not boyfriend material?"

"No more anything. I don't think I can trust him."

Once he'd finished eating, Celeste said, "Show me the photos."

With the food in his belly, Truman was starting to feel more energetic. He rose and dumped the containers in the garbage, then went to grab his laptop and a couple of the Italian sodas from the fridge. When he came back to the sofa, he handed a bottle to Celeste and sat down, pulling open his computer.

The memory card, he remembered. Rising again, he strode over to his clothes rack and dug in the pocket of his rust-colored pants, lying rumpled in the laundry basket with his other dirty clothes. The little black rectangle was still there, caught in the folded layers of sticky tape. Back at the sofas, he sat and spent a minute carefully peeling the tape apart to free the card.

"Dyson had it stuck to the bottom of a drawer," Truman explained.

"That sounds like a clever hiding place. Better than in an easily stolen book."

"I hope the photos are actually on this thing."

Celeste frowned. "Do you think Dyson is playing you?"

"He lied to me before. Biff Sturgis says you have to assume that everyone is lying all the time. The only truth is in the evidence itself."

Once the card was free, Truman slid it into the slot in his laptop and clicked open the folder with the photos. Celeste got up and sat beside him to see the screen.

"Whoa," she said, startled at the first image that popped up. It was a crowd of about a dozen men dressed in jeans and brown shirts, walking on a dirt road, but what popped out was the lurid red of the German swastika flag.

"Look at the trees," Truman said. "That's definitely somewhere temperate like Oregon."

The next photo was almost the same, and the next. A few of the images were closer, depicting the marchers from the waist up. Once he'd clicked rapidly through them all, Truman zoomed in on the faces in the first image.

"That's Irwin Jeffries," Celeste said, pointing at one of them. "He's a lot younger, but there's no mistaking him."

In one of the images, the men were all shouting simultaneously, baring their teeth like angry dogs. In another image Irwin was smiling and looking off to the side.

"There's no way he could deny being part of this group," Truman said. "He's not the one carrying the Nazi flag, but he's dressed the same as everyone else."

"Whoever shot these was a skilled photographer," Celeste said. "He knew about composition."

"The color looks a little weird, though. Like the film has deteriorated."

"Color negative technology changed in the 1970s. Prints from older film never looked quite right."

Truman eyed her. "You studied photography too?"

"Not at school, but it's part of the art world. The switch in the color process is really useful for dating prints made from negatives. It makes me think these are older than Dyson assumed. He said 1980s, but I'd bet it was early or mid-1970s."

"Irwin can't be much over thirty here," Truman said.

"That fits, considering his age now." Celeste reached for the computer, then zoomed in on an image. "I can tell you more. Look at the graininess when you get in close. That's idiosyncratic to film. It went away with digital. This isn't too grainy, so it was a fast film, meant for use in daylight." She zoomed out again. "See how the trees look really close behind them? That means the photographer was standing some distance away and using a telephoto lens."

"Maybe he was spying on them," Truman said. "Although when you march around with a flag and shout stuff, you're kind of asking for attention."

"Maybe the photographer just didn't want to be in the middle of it. You get better candid images when you stand back, because the subjects aren't focused on the camera. But you might be right. Maybe they didn't even know he was there. None of them are looking at the camera in any of these shots."

Truman sat back. "So what do we do with this? If we distribute it, we'll burn down his business, and your new crush will be unemployed."

"The business will be fine. But it might burn down Irwin Jeffries."

"Are we sure we want to do that? If it were about me, I wouldn't want to be judged by things I did a lifetime ago."

Celeste clicked on a photo. "Look at him, Tru. He's marching with a Nazi flag."

"It's been a long time. Maybe he's reformed."

"The first thing he asked me when we met was what country I was from. I'm from this country, just as much as he is, but I'm brown, so in his worldview I don't count. He also called a business associate a Chinaman. The guy is from Gardena. And that's just the racist component of the whole vile package—he called me a dummy, and honey, and sugar."

"I get it," Truman said. "His views haven't changed. He's also screwing over the people on the streets of Skid Row—the people he was given a tax break to help."

"I vote that Irwin Jeffries needs to go down," Celeste said.

He nodded. "Agreed."

They spent a few hours formulating a plan, and when they had it all hammered out, Celeste rose and stretched.

"I need to get some sleep," she said. "Are we absolutely sure we can trust the contralto with this?"

"She hasn't lied to me yet. Dyson says people with nothing have a raw kind of honesty."

"I guess we'll find out."

Celeste gave him an air kiss and then went down to her car. The alley was quiet, she saw, glancing toward the shadowy tents as she got behind the wheel. Pulling out, she stifled a yawn and headed for home. Let's hope this works.

SEVENTEEN

In the morning Truman had his coffee and got dressed, then went down to the street and into the alley, instinctively breathing through his mouth to avoid the stench as he stepped in among the tents.

"Angel," he shouted, then paused to listen. There was no response. "Hey, Beretta."

A few yards away, emerging slowly from behind a tent, naked from the waist up, like a ratty and beat-up version of Venus rising from the sea foam, Beretta appeared, his hair tied behind his head.

"Good morning, Sunshine," Beretta said, and rolled his shoulders, concentrating on the action, as if they were stiff. "You look especially pretty today."

"That's very sweet of you to say," Truman said, his brow furrowing. "Have you seen Angel?"

"She left a while ago. I'll let her know you're looking for her."

"Tell her to ring my doorbell. I have some money for her."

He spread his arms wide. "You can just leave it with me."

"Thanks, Beretta," Truman said, and turned to walk back out to the street, then up to his loft.

The buzzer sounded not long after, and Truman trotted down to the front door.

"Hey, Sunshine," Angel said, a big smile on her face. She was wearing jeans and the same lightweight jacket she always wore, with the torn shoulder. "What's this I hear about cash money?"

"I have a job for you. Are you busy this evening?"

"What kind of job?"

"You'd be crashing a meeting," Truman said, and gave her an outline of the plan. "It'll be a bunch of white guys."

She held up a palm. "Angel is not afraid of white folks."

"You might have to be a little aggressive."

"Most people assume crazy is my baseline," she said. "This sounds like entry-level crazy."

"It's also possible that you might get detained."

"Will there be cops?"

"That's unlikely. Maybe a bouncer, or a security guard."

"Angel knows how not to get detained. It's about making yourself loud and unmanageable, to the point that they just want you gone. It doesn't fly with the police, but it works flawlessly in the retail setting."

Truman grinned at that. "So you're interested?"

"How much are you paying?"

"How much do you want?"

Angel pursed her lips and looked thoughtful. "Well, to carry out a complex operation like this, I'd need to get paid a hundred dollars."

"I can do that."

"I'm not going to get popped, but if I do get popped, will you bail me out?"

"Of course," Truman said. "I'd go directly to the jailhouse and bang on the doors."

"That's not how it works," Angel said, eyeing him dubiously. "So what time is the meeting?"

"Later, but we need to prepare. Celeste is coming over soon. Will you be in the alley?"

"I'll be around. I'll watch for her car."

———•———

Celeste spent the morning at home, researching portable action cameras. Once she understood the basics, she climbed in her car and drove to a sporting-goods store along a commercial street in her neighborhood. The place was quiet this early in the day. The clerk was a lean guy with a great pomp. He couldn't have been much older than twenty, and he was happy to show her the cameras.

"Which one works best in low light?" Celeste asked.

The clerk picked up one of the sturdy-looking little boxes and explained the features.

"I need to mount it on my clothes," Celeste said, looking over the device. "How do we do that?"

"What kind of activity is it for?"

"Uh—hiking."

"We have helmet mounts, but you probably don't wear a helmet when you're hiking. There's also a chest-strap mount. Do you carry a back-pack or a day pack?"

"I don't."

He frowned. "So you could get a rock-climb-ing harness that goes around your shoulders like a backpack. It's not meant specifically for a cam-era, but I bet it'll work." He went to get one, and returned a moment later to demonstrate it for her.

Made of dark-red nylon, the harness went on like a bra, and the clerk attached the camera to it with velcro straps. Once she'd adjusted the har-ness, the device was positioned right below her collarbone, free of her cleavage.

"This works fine," Celeste said. "Do you have one in black?"

He did, and a few minutes later she'd paid for it, and the camera, and headed out to her car.

Pulling up in front of Truman's loft, she pressed the buzzer and went upstairs. Just as she stepped inside, the buzzer sounded again.

"That'll be Angel," Truman said. "She said she'd watch for your car."

"I'll go down," Celeste said. "Hopefully we'll be back soon." She handed him the bag with the camera in it, then went back down the stairs.

Angel greeted her as she pushed out the front door.

"It's the pretty lady."

"It's the contralto," Celeste said. "You'll need a dress for tonight."

"I don't have any of those."

"So let's go buy you one."

"This is the right neighborhood," Angel said, waving at the street. "There are a thousand clothing stores around here."

"Do you mind wearing used stuff?"

Angel frowned, then held up a finger and waggled it. "Girl—Angel is not that proud."

"So we'll drive," Celeste said, and opened the passenger door for her.

The closest thrift store she knew was a big one just outside downtown, on the other side of the freeway. As she drove, Angel asked her a series of questions about what she was supposed to do, exactly, at Jeffries's meeting. Talking it through with her made Celeste more confident about the operation—Angel understood the plan, and the things she was asking were lucid and reasonable.

Celeste pulled into the parking lot of the thrift store, and they went inside, heading to the women's section, where the dresses filled several racks. As she was flipping through the options, she heard Angel cackle behind her, and turned to look.

"Check this out," Angel said, holding up a red gingham dress with a tight waist and a flared skirt. "Isn't this great? It'll fit me."

"If you were going on a hayride, I'd say that was a great choice," Celeste said. "We need something in black."

Eventually she found one that looked right, and handed it to Angel, who stepped over to the mirror and held it up in front of her.

"It's a little somber," Angel said, "but not bad."

"Try it on."

She watched Angel open her jacket to hold the waist of the dress against her own. While she was waiting, Celeste dug around in her bag for that half trank that she knew was still there. Eventually she found it, and popped it in her mouth.

"Do you have one of those for me?" Angel said, watching her in the mirror.

"It's not recreational. It's my medication."

"Oh, yeah? What kind of medication?"

"Birth control," Celeste said flatly.

Angel arched her eyebrows. "Whatever you say. But I know you're not getting busy with Sunshine. He's not that type."

Celeste waved at the dress. "Are you going to try that on?"

"I don't need to. It'll fit." She turned to face her. "If I'm wearing this, I'll need hair."

"So let's go find you some," Celeste said, and took the dress from her, and went to pay for it at the register.

Once they were in the car again, she checked her phone for wig places. There was one in a strip mall just a few blocks away.

Celeste parked out front, and the pair of them went inside. It was a narrow space with shelves of wigs on white foam heads stacked up to the ceiling. Angel ogled all the options.

"Such pretty things," she murmured.

The clerk, an elderly woman, came to the counter. Celeste greeted her and eyed her hair. She was definitely wearing some of her own inventory.

"Let me try that one," Angel said, pointing to a black shoulder-length cascade of curls.

The clerk handed her a nylon skull cap, then carefully lifted the wig off its perch. Angel knew the drill, and quickly had the cap over her own hair. Once she had the mass of curls properly positioned, she shook her head and pawed at her bangs.

"How does it look?" Angel said.

"It's a lot of hair," Celeste said. It was also twenty years too young for her, and decades out of style, but she didn't say that. "It looks perfect." She turned to the clerk. "How much is it?"

"That's one of our deluxe models," the woman said. "The ultra-full-length line. It's a little more than most."

"OK," Celeste said, and raised her eyebrows.

"Thirty-nine ninety-nine, plus tax."

Celeste nodded and dug out her cash, suppressing a smile. That kind of deluxe was completely painless.

EIGHTEEN

On his computer, Truman picked the photos from Dyson's memory card that showed Jeffries's youthful face most clearly, then spent some time on them with photo-editing software. First he superimposed a red arrow, pointed at his head, and added IRWIN JEFFRIES in bold red letters. It didn't even need annotation, as it was so obviously him—the jawline was the same, and the eyes, and even though his hair had since gone gray, he still wore it in the same slicked-back style.

Truman printed out a dozen sets of the photos and stapled them in one corner. His printer didn't do high-quality images, but they were clear, and in color, so the red in the Nazi flag really popped.

The door buzzer sounded, and Truman

pressed the button to unlock it, then flipped open his deadbolt. Angel and Celeste stepped in a moment later, shopping bags in hand. Angel looked around at his loft.

"This is just elegant."

"Thanks," Truman said. It wasn't, he knew that, but to a homeless person it might look like paradise.

"Can I use your bathroom?" Angel said.

"Of course."

She stepped inside the little room, then stuck her head out. "Can I take a shower?"

"Why not?" Truman said. "Let me find you a towel."

"There's already one in here."

"That's the one I use," he said, but she had already closed the door.

"This is why you don't sleep with homeless people," Celeste said. "Your water bill goes through the roof."

"I'm glad we got started early."

Truman listened as the water started to run, and they waited on the sofas as the smell of soap and the mist from Angel's luxuriously lengthy shower wafted through the loft. Celeste thumbed through the printouts Truman had made, then tapped at the bright-red annotations.

"Flint is going to hate me."

"You're not the one marching around with a

Nazi flag," Truman said. "Like you said last night, this is aimed at Irwin."

"Still, Flint wasn't anticipating anything like this. It feels like a betrayal."

"If he doesn't like the truth about his father, that's his problem. You're barely even the messenger."

"But I am like a spy."

At that moment Angel reappeared, wrapped in Truman's towel. She looked relaxed and happy.

"Let's try on the dress," Celeste said, rising from the sofa.

"There's nowhere to change."

"Behind the clothes rack," Truman said.

Celeste went over and rolled it out from the wall. "I love that this thing has wheels."

Angel stepped behind the rack and reappeared a minute later in the black dress. The neckline showed a lot of shoulder, and the hem hung below her knees.

"It fits you pretty well," Celeste said, hands on her hips, assessing her.

"You look amazing," Truman said.

"Where's my hair?"

Celeste handed her the bag, and Angel pulled on the wig, deftly flicking the curls away from her face, as if she'd always had them.

"It all works," Celeste said.

Truman murmured agreement. "We should

fit you with the camera."

"I have to take pictures?" Angel said, frowning.

"It's a video camera," Celeste said, stepping over to Truman's desk to retrieve the bag that bore the logo of the sporting goods store. "You just have to wear it."

She helped Angel put on the camera harness, and adjust the fit, and then position the device.

"It totally blends in," Truman said. "The black straps on the black dress. In a dimly lit room, no one will even notice it."

"Let's get it connected to my phone," Celeste said, and pulled it out.

Angel flipped her hair with a hand and eyed Truman. "What have you got to eat around here?"

"Cereal," he said. "Some fruit. Maybe a granola bar. Half a cucumber."

"We can order some hot food," Celeste said.

Angel beamed. "That sounds lovely."

"Who delivers here?" Celeste asked him.

"Thai, or pizza, or burritos."

"Let's have a pizza," Angel said.

Truman pulled out his phone. "What do you want on it?"

She frowned in thought. "Olives—the black ones … cheese, of course … mushrooms."

Truman nodded as he tapped at his phone. He chose vegan cheese, as nobody would notice the difference. Angel asked for pepperoni too, but no way was Truman paying for meat.

"Thirty minutes," he said, and tucked his phone away.

Celeste spent some time setting up the camera, pressing its buttons and working with her phone. Eventually she called Angel over and put the camera back in the harness. Truman stood beside Celeste's to look at the screen. It took him a moment to realize he was looking at himself, standing beside Celeste in his own loft. Her phone was showing a live video stream from Angel's perspective.

"Walk around a little," Celeste said.

Angel swanned around the big room, pausing now and then to pose like a model on the runway, hands planted on her hips, elbows spread wide, chin in the air.

"It's working fine," Celeste said finally. "The software even compensates for uneven movement."

"Is it recording the video stream too?"

Celeste tapped at her phone. "It's all here."

"It doesn't need Wi-Fi?"

"I added it to my data plan. That's why it had to be linked to my phone specifically. I guess it could get expensive if it uploads a lot of video."

"Let's hope a few minutes in that steak house is all we need."

The door buzzer sounded, and Truman went

down to the front entrance to get the pizza, tipping the delivery driver a fin. Back upstairs, he set the box on the counter next to the sink, and each of them took a slice.

"They forgot the pepperoni," Angel said.

Truman studied his slice. "That's so weird."

Angel had another piece, and when neither of them went for more, asked, "Can I take the rest?"

"It's all yours," Truman said. "I'll wrap it in foil."

"So I know what I'm supposed to do," Angel said, turning to Celeste, "but I'd like to practice."

"Let's sit down, and we'll go through it," Celeste said, leading her to the sofas.

Truman joined them once the rest of the pizza was in the fridge, and they coached Angel on her mission.

"How do I find the right table?"

"They'll be in a private back room." Truman rose and held out his hands, drawing a door frame in the air in front of him. "Here's the front entrance from the street." He walked through it and stopped, then gestured to the right. "Here's the host's stand. There's a bar on this side, and tables on the left. You keep walking through." He took a few more steps. "The way into the kitchen is here, and over here is a doorway into the back room." He mimed it in front of him. "It has a black curtain, not a door, so you can just walk in."

"Got it," Angel said. "All the way back, then through the curtain on the left."

"How do you know the layout?" Celeste said.

Truman shrugged. "I looked online. There are tons of selfies and review photos."

"Do you want to do a run-through?" Celeste said, eyeing Angel.

She leapt up and walked through the steps Truman had modeled, narrating her path. When she got to the imagined back room, she threw the curtains wide and gave an intense performance.

"I think your approach is right," Celeste said. "Don't be afraid to raise your voice."

"Angel is no shrinking violet," she said, waving a hand.

"They should be there by now," Truman said, glancing at his phone. "We should go."

Angel took a deep breath. "I'm ready. Should we all have a stiff drink first?"

"No," Truman said flatly.

Celeste checked the camera in its harness and gently adjusted Angel's voluminous hair. Truman grabbed the photo printouts and followed them down the stairs.

Angel sat on the passenger's side of Celeste's little car, and Truman climbed in the backseat. The restaurant wasn't far, on the other side of downtown, and soon Celeste was driving in front of it, cruising past the valet stand.

"That's the place," Angel said, pointing out the window.

"You're right," Truman said, glad that she was so sharp right now.

Celeste pulled into a loading zone a few doors farther down.

"You don't think we'll get eighty-sixed from here?" he said.

"It's Saturday evening, and most of this block is offices. No one is going to be using the yellow curb."

"So we'll be right here when you get back," he said to Angel.

"Camera on." Celeste reached for it on Angel's chest and pressed the power button. She glanced at her phone to make sure it was transmitting the image, then added, "We're live."

Truman rolled the printouts into a cylinder and handed them up to Angel. "Ready to go?"

"I'm ready," she said, her voice loud, and smacked the dashboard with the rolled-up paper. She climbed out and strutted back down the street toward the restaurant.

Truman got out and watched her step inside, then sat in the front seat and cranked the window down a few inches. Celeste held her phone between them so they could both watch the feed from the camera.

In the video image, a guy with a little mustache

and thinning hair appeared. His eyes focused above the camera, and he flashed a thin smile.

"That must be the maître d'," Truman said.

His expression shifted as he slid out of the frame.

"I'm with the party in the back," Angel said.

The bar went by on the right, a blur of bottles and dark wood. Angel was moving quickly. She weaved around a waiter, then the screen went black as she stepped up to the curtain and entered the back room. A moment later the camera adjusted to the low light, and the image stabilized.

"She's in," Celeste said.

On the screen was a round table draped in white and covered with plates and glasses and bottles. Jeffries was on the left side, one of maybe six people seated around it. It looked like they were in the middle of a meal.

"I have some handouts for this meeting," Angel said, her voice booming. The table loomed larger, and paper fluttered in the image as she handed a set of printouts to the closest person.

"How much is Jeffries paying y'all?" Angel demanded.

"She sounds all Southern now," Truman said.

"She said she had people in Louisiana, remember?" Celeste said. "Maybe she's channeling them."

Angel set a sheaf of paper in front of the next

man at the table, who recoiled as she approached.

"What's your name, *flaco?*" Angel said. "Are you in the zoning department, or is it planning?"

"This is a private meeting," someone said sharply.

"That's the problem," Angel said, raising her voice as she made her way around the table. "This kind of skulduggery needs some sunshine."

Gazing at the video feed, Celeste chuckled. "Did she just say 'skulduggery'?"

"Y'all can take his money," Angel shouted, "but you can't keep it a secret. Skid Row will rise again."

She was in front of Jeffries now, who sat there glaring at her, murder in his eyes. Behind him a beefy guy with a black jacket and a security guard's badge stepped into the frame, and hustled toward her, stepping behind Jeffries's chair. The camera jerked and the image went dark as he grabbed her arms.

"Hey! Don't you put your hands on a sister," Angel shouted, and then louder, "Y'all pay attention! The contralto has sung."

The guard must have spun her around, because the camera's view was clear again. Jeffries was in front of her, on his feet now, his face visibly red even in the low light.

"Get the camera," Jeffries said through his teeth.

A hand went over the lens, and there was the sound of ripping velcro. A moment later the image stopped moving, and fixed on a close-up view of the curving edge of a plate and a wineglass stem.

Angel's voice was farther away now, and growing fainter. "Hey! Fire!" she cried. "Help! … Murder!"

"That's what I'd call making a scene," Truman said.

The image moved again, a jumble of motion, for a moment showing Jeffries's angry face as he glared directly at the lens. Another blur of motion and the image went black, the audio suddenly muffled.

"That's it," Truman said. "He put it in his pocket."

"I guess I won't be returning that to the store."

"At least we got the video."

They could hear Angel now, without the camera, audible through the car's open window.

"That's assault, you sick motherfucker," she shouted. "You don't get to grope my breasts."

In the side mirror Truman could see her now, marching away from the restaurant. The big guy with the security badge followed her a few steps but then stopped, watching her go.

"Start the engine," Truman said.

"I'm so glad they didn't try to detain her."

"Angel told me it's a tactic—you get louder so

that they just want you out."

"It makes sense," Celeste said. "If they tried to keep her there until the cops came, she might be able to charge them with assault, or unlawful detention. Angel knows what she's doing."

As she strode up to the car, Truman reached back and popped open the rear door. Angel climbed in, and as soon as the door slammed, Celeste revved the engine and pulled out, pushing the little car as fast as it could go with the weight of three people in it.

"The security guard watched me leave, but I don't think we have a tail," Angel said, looking out the rear window. She turned around and leaned between the seats. "I'm so sorry, honey— they took your camera."

"It doesn't matter," Celeste said. "We recorded the video from it."

"You were freaking brilliant," Truman said, and held up his palm.

Angel smacked it in a high five and whooped "woo-hoo!" To Celeste, she said, "Girlfriend— hands up for a sister."

"I can't while I'm driving," Celeste said, and laughed. "You're a natural-born performer."

"Oh, you know it."

Angel squeezed her shoulder and sat back, dancing with her arms and flipping her hair. She was amped up, Truman saw, watching her with a big smile on his face. It would take a few minutes for that to wear off.

"Who is the soul queen?" Angel demanded.

"It's all about Angel," Truman said. "All soul queen, all the time."

She let out another whoop. Celeste laughed and congratulated her, managing to keep her eyes on the road.

By the time they pulled up at Truman's loft, the adrenaline was waning for all of them, and they were quieter as they trudged up the stairs.

"I should change," Angel said, and walked over behind Truman's clothes rack.

"You can keep the dress," Celeste called to her. "The hair too."

When Angel appeared again, she looked ready for the street, in her baggy jeans and jacket. Truman handed her a soda, and the three of them tapped their bottles together.

"Did you get all the pictures you needed?" Angel said, after she'd taken a long drink.

"We'll go through it later," Truman said, "but I think so."

"I know you got clear images of the faces of some of those sleazy bureaucrats, at least," Celeste said. "We watched from the car."

"I'm glad to hear it," Angel said, and drained her bottle. "I should go. Where's my wages, and my pizza?"

Truman went to the fridge to retrieve the leftovers, and Celeste dug in her bag, producing a sheaf of twenties. As Truman watched, she counted out twenty-five of them—five hundred bucks.

"That's so generous," Angel said, quickly pocketing the wad of cash. "Celeste, your little car has permanent protection from now on. I won't let Beretta or any of those goons break into it."

"Does Beretta break into cars?" Truman said.

Angel eyed him and spoke gravely. "I can neither confirm nor deny that information at this time."

Celeste scoffed. "You sound like you work for your Uncle Sam."

Angel waved dismissively. "All I can say is, don't leave anything of value in view." She tucked the leftover pizza into the plastic bag with the dress and the wig.

Truman followed her to the door to bolt it after her.

"Don't be a stranger, Sunshine," she said as she left.

"I hope the five wasn't excessive," Celeste said.

"I was going to give her a hundred. That's what she asked for. I figured I'd give her more later, so it wouldn't all get blown at once."

"You're not her father, and she's not at addict."

"I didn't want to turn her into one either."

Celeste sighed. "Anyway, it's done. We've got work to do."

They sat together on one of the sofas and pulled open Truman's laptop. First Celeste copied the video recording to his computer, then deleted everything from the cloud, and removed the camera from her cell phone account.

"It's gone," she said. "I hope that means Jeffries can't trace it to me."

"He'll probably be able to, if he wants to. You weren't the one who went in there, so your story is that the camera got stolen from your car today, soon after you bought it. You didn't make a police report because it wasn't worth that much."

Celeste nodded. "Smart. It would be hard to disprove."

Next, they went through the video. The quality was consistent, and it was clear what was happening, except when the guard started to manhandle Angel.

"You can see this guy's face pretty clearly," Truman said, pausing it for a moment, then letting it play. "The next one too. He looks a little shocked."

"Maybe they'll think twice before dining out with Irwin Jeffries again."

The talked about how to edit the video, and finally agreed to cut out the part before Angel entered the back room, and then end the clip after Jeffries pocketed the camera. Truman copied the video file into a cloud folder with the photos of the neo-Nazi rally.

"I'll send links to share it from my secondary email," he said. "It doesn't have my real name."

"What media outlets would even look at this?" Celeste said.

They talked it through, and compiled a list, and spent some time finding the right email addresses. Truman also sent it to the anti-gentrification group that had spoken out against A Cut Above, and to Dyson, and to Ivy.

"What about the paper?" Celeste said.

"They're in bed with guys like Jeffries. They'll never print it."

"Of course not. But if everyone else in town publishes it, they'll want to report on that." She lowered her voice to mimic a news broadcast. "'We don't report trash, but we'll tell you when someone else does.'"

Truman nodded and spent a minute finding a couple of names to send the link to.

"You know," Celeste said, "using an email with a pseudonym isn't really going to protect you. A decent journalist will be able to trace it to you pretty quickly."

"I know that's a possibility. If the story blows up, maybe it's inevitable."

"It means your name is going to be connected to this story."

"So I'll have to do some interviews."

"That's not the issue," she said. "You're making some powerful enemies."

"You think Jeffries is going to sue me for damages? I guess he could get a few hundred bucks if the court seized my electronics and sold my good shoes, but otherwise I don't have a lot to lose."

"Your life, Truman," she said intently.

"If Jeffries didn't ice Dyson, he won't come for me either. There's nothing worse I can do to him than what we just did. He'll leave me alone."

"What about the bureaucrats? They could sic the cops on you."

"Hopefully their instinct will be to lie low for a while. If there's media attention on them, they'll be motivated to behave."

"Still, it sucks that they're getting away with it." Celeste sighed and sat back. "I wish we could get them indicted for taking bribes."

"On what evidence? Video of a homeless woman dancing around a restaurant? Nothing will come of it legally. But maybe Jeffries and the city will be embarrassed into keeping their word about Skid Row housing."

"I guess we've done all we can."

"With a little help from Angel," Truman said.

Celeste nodded. "The contralto has sung."

Also from Dagmar Miura

The Margarita Solution

In the first novel in the Truman and Celeste series, Truman stumbles into a detective gig and Celeste works her contacts in the art world as they wrangle with a series of lowlifes and some toxic secrets.

truman.dagmarmiura.com

Chiseler with a Glass Jaw

Never one to let a bully get away with harassing someone, Celeste intervenes with a knockout punch, and in the melee Truman winds up in possession of the bully's cell phone. Through inventive online stalking, the boozy duo uncovers a seedy nest of grifters.

celeste.dagmarmiura.com

The Slater Ibáñez Books

Don't mess with the hothead—or he might just mess with you. Slater is only interested in two kinds of guys: the ones he wants to punch, and the ones he sleeps with. Things get interesting when they start to overlap.

slater.dagmarmiura.com

The Mason Braithwaite Paranormal Mystery Series

No one is ever quite sure whether psychic investigator Mason gets results with actual psychic power or his more mundane flatfooting, but the disheveled redhead manages to resolve some intractable mysteries.

mason.dagmarmiura.com

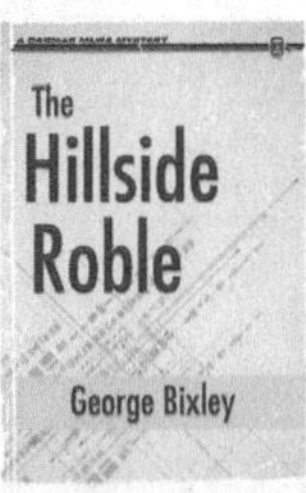

The Hillside Roble

Investigating a million-dollar heist at a gallery in the Arts District, Slater can't get a face-to-face with the owner, Eli, until he applies a little pressure. Eli turns out to be a minor celebrity, physically flawless but obsessed with his own image, and flaky in that uniquely LA way.

slater.dagmarmiura.com

Penstock Canyon

While helping out a friend suffering from late-night visitations, psychic investigator Mason is confronted with aliens on the roof and other liminal beings that have him questioning the very nature of reality.

mason.dagmarmiura.com

The Bone Bridge

Yarrott Benz, the 2016 Ippy Award winner for memoir, is forced to deal with extraordinary self-sacrifice in this harrowing account of teenage brothers, as different as night and day, trapped together in a dramatic medical dilemma.

bonebridge.dagmarmiura.com

The Psychic Vegan Cookbook

It has never been easier to cook vegan, and you don't even need to be psychic to do it. Whether your motivation is eating healthier or the welfare of other sentient creatures, Henrietta Flores guides you through plant-based versions of familiar dishes.

cookbook.dagmarmiura.com

www.ingramcontent.com/pod-product-compliance
Lightning Source LLC
Chambersburg PA
CBHW010348170726
48284CB00011B/2829